# Huntley Haverstock
## The Reluctant Spy

By Freddy King

# Table of Contents

# <u>Chapter 1</u>

Freddy Goodchild was born in the north eastern industrial town of Middlesbrough, in the middle of the Second World War. He was an only child. His world was Park Lane and the surrounding streets and near a park opened and championed by Prince Albert husband of Queen Victoria. The houses were built in the nineteenth century for workers in the local industries. At his young age everything seemed vast including the park which had areas where places appeared mysterious. From his bedroom window he could see over the high wall opposite his house into the maternity hospital. The gardens were beautifully kept by the resident gardener and beyond he could see the trees and open spaces of Albert Park. He spend many happy hours playing with the local boys on the hill called Bell's Hill in the park, probably named after the bell that had been placed at the top of the hill.

He was quite small for his age but he was very popular with the local children. His home was nearly always deserted as his family members were frequently absent, which is why he spent so much time away from his house. In those times it was not unusual for children to be left alone as very few came to mishap. The house was an old, rented, Victorian, corner, town house built during the early establishment of the industrial environment in the North East of England. The Steel Works were a major employer in Middlesbrough. The property was a 'two up, two down' building but with a totally abandoned second floor that at some time had been a bathroom and a bedroom that was under the sloping roof of the house but was now in a sad state of repair. The upper house had been abandoned for some time and was just bare dusty boards on the floor and no furniture of any sort.

At the junction outside of the house was a large re-enforced concrete community bomb shelter and in the front garden was an Anderson bomb shelter. As well as the bomb shelters the house and back yard were excellent places to play without interruption or observation from adult intervention. His father was never known by him and the mother never lived down the shame of an unmarried pregnancy but the shame was purely in his mother's mind. Many of the local girls had been left alone with a child for a variety of reasons. War time was like that.

Without a father and a mother who would not

speak of any father or any mentor from family or friends, he grew up self reliant and street wise. The home was only a place to sleep or play when empty and his education was acquired from his peer group and the related groups of down town urchins. The war left the town scarred through the frequent attempts by the German air force to bomb the steel and chemical works that provided the main employment and income for the town. The industry provided a massive contribution to the British war effort. All the metal garden gates and railings had been smelted down for arms and bullets at the local iron and steel works. The bomb damage to the local area was a perfect play ground for the youngsters. Even the town centre had been heavily bombed and many of the main stores were just open cellars after the rubble had been cleared.

The air raid shelters were used as dens and the bombed houses were great for hide and seek. Freddy Goodchild, as a very young child, spent his days in the local nursery where many of his happier memories were located. His mother earned a meager living as a 'Clippy' on the buses. The varied shifts of the work pattern meant that his mother was very rarely at home for significant periods of time. When she was at home the number of 'uncles' that visited the house were beyond the understanding of young Freddy but the gifts that he received from uncles, given to 'go and play', were very welcome and Freddy was only too pleased to oblige. One 'uncle Freddy' gave him a heavy overcoat and in the pocket was a half crown. In those days half a crown was a fortune. On that occasion he was, of course, told to leave the house and go and show all of his friends his new coat. He was surprised at the number of family members that came to visit and he was surprised at the large family to which he appeared to be a part. Strangely he never saw the associated Aunties.

His time at nursery school was a joy for him. Nurse Pallister was one of the nursery staff and she became a substitute mother figure for him. The nursery was located at the end of Park Lane through the only gate in the high wall that stretched the length of the lane. It was a very private and beautifully appointed nursey for children from all backgrounds but restricted to only twenty in number. Those were his memorable happy days of that time of his life. In later years he frequently visited the elderly Nurse Pallister who was always very interested in Freddy's activities and progress.

Freddy left the nursery school and moved on to the local primary school at Victoria Road. and his education on the subject of girls blossomed. The school was built by the Victorians and it was a solid old building with a playground within high brick walls. The upper school was privileged with a steel posted fence that gave a view through the bars to Victoria Road and the outside world. The school rooms had windows well above the height of any occupant in the building, ensuring that there was no distraction by the outside world. Celia was just one of the attractive girls who seemed fascinated by the difference between the sexes and Freddy learned that his genitals were not just for physical comfort. Celia seemed to get great pleasure from handling Freddy's parts under the desk whilst the teacher attempted to impart knowledge at the blackboard. This activity did, in fact, cause some distraction from the teaching. Billy went to school with Freddy and they frequently met at Billy's house. The house was about fifty yards and around the corner from Freddy's house in Granville Road.

His parents like Freddy's were always working until late at one of the local hostelries. They worked at the Westminster Pub on Parliament Road and Billy had the run of the house just about every evening. His older brothers had girl friends around on a regular basis, all in party mood and Celia was a guest of Freddy's on many occasions. That was the time that Freddy realized what was happening at his house after hearing and seeing the upstairs activities and the knowledge made him feel even more isolated.

When his mother married, it was to a very new 'uncle' called Peter who was a bus driver at the bus depot where she worked. Peter was a dour soul and he had a very limited sense of humour, I suppose that one could call him a typical simple yorkshireman, simple being the operative word. Peter was from a quite large family with relations all over the County of Yorkshire. His uncle Jack was the head reader at the Yorkshire Post newspaper. Jack lived directly opposite the Headingly cricket ground and matches could be seen and followed from the upstairs front room. In his teenage years many a happy time was spent there watching Yorkshire cricketers take on the best teams in the country.

The wedding was paid for by the groom's parents and they insisted on a church wedding. It was all very grand but Freddy was not invited. He was an embarrassment for his mother as she was being wed in white. This fact was vehemently referred to by Freddy's grandmother to all persons that she encountered. It was only years later that

Freddy found out that his grandmother had never been married. The wedding was obviously not a love match as the number of visiting uncles did not diminish and there was obvious resentment from Peter towards another man's child in his marriage. Arguments frequently occurred at home and Freddy's parents did not talk to each other for weeks on end. They communicated through terse notes left for each other to find. The atmosphere at home was quite toxic for a lot of the time. Freddy became the ball to be kicked to and fro during the frantic discussions.

Freddy spent most of his time outside of the home playing in bomb damaged buildings and the Anderson and Communal air raid shelters that still remained after the war. They were usually in poor condition, with a foot of water in the bases of the Anderson shelters and varied refuse left after the many activities that occurred in the Communal shelters. Life changed radically when they left his grandfather's rented house in Park Lane and moved into a brand new house on a council estate at Beechwood.

The house was on the south side of the estate and facing open countryside. The fields, trees and streams were a revelation to Freddy. He had never seen greenery outside of the local park which, to him, was real countryside, as it was surrounded by railings, even though it was sternly patrolled by a very grumpy and intolerant Park Keeper. The window from his bedroom gave views, not of high walls and fences but of distant hills and farm lands, cows, sheep and horses. The horses astounded him. He had seen the local coal man on his cart delivering his loads of coal but the horses from his window were sleek, powerful animals which were totally different from the heavy, tired, lumbering beasts of burden that he was used to seeing. The Lamp Lighter no longer came round the roads riding his bicycle with his long pole to turn on the gas and light the gas filament with the flame at the end of his pole. The electric lights came on as if by magic. It was a wild and massive new playground which afforded every opportunity to spend lots of time away from the house and the discord atmosphere in there.

Now only the most persistent one or two uncles came and went. Just over a year later, Freddy passed the scholarship, the eleven plus and elected to go to the only real grammar school in the area. The only response that he got from home was 'how did you manage that?' Acklam Hall Grammar School was three miles away from the estate across open fields and streams, some occupied by cows and sometimes bulls. Freddy learned not to dawdle when crossing fields and his ability and speed for running developed. The bull population was very fast for their size. The headmaster had very little time for council estate students and took every opportunity to embarrass or punish any child with that background. Freddy took his revenge on the headmaster in his final year when the decorators arrived to cover the work of the student toilet artists and school wits. The head appeared to be a funny purple colour as he climbed on stage at the final morning assembly.

The whole School was totally aware of recent happenings and were trying very hard not to explode into laughter as the head spluttered out his disapproval and vague threats against the perpetrators. He had arrived at his prestigious and historic school to find 'Joe's Cafe' painted, in six-foot-high capital letters, on the roof. It could be seen for miles, glowing in the twilight and glaring in the day's sunlight advertising the school to all far and wide. The black knickers and brassieres hoisted up to the top of the flag pole did nothing to sweeten his mood on the last day of term. The underwear had been kindly donated by girls from the adjacent all girls school. Some of the governors were ex students and found the whole incident hilarious. The final day was Presentation Day and the Governors took the stage for the awards. After the awards it was the custom to congratulate the school and its' students on the year's achievements but the Chair of Governors could not resist a mildly supportive comment towards the culprits. They had a sneaky feeling of admiration wishing that they had thought of it when they were students. Freddy left the school with a respectable number of 'O' and 'A' levels at GCE. Freddy's parents were too busy with their own lives to even comment on his final report.

# **<u>Chapter 2</u>**

His mother's brother, Derek, had joined the Royal Air Force some years before and always promoted an exciting image with photographs of himself with his buddies during the Suez crisis. One story came from a picture sent from Egypt of Derek and his buddies in the desert near the Suez Canal with a detail on the picture of a round black mark on Derek's chest. His note was to confirm it was a print error and not a bullet hole. Freddy was truly impressed with the photographs and took the opportunity on leaving school and after a variety of casual employments, he joined up and became an airman. He wanted to be a pilot and applied for aircrew. The basic aircrew training was undertaken by all applicants and selection for aircrew posts was a one day aptitude assessment.

Things did not go well for the selection. Freddy was delayed by administrative duties. He told the duty officer about the selection times but the officer was Administration Staff and resented the 'Brylcream boys' and their rapid promotion, so he was as awkward as possible. The selection and the pilot familiarisation had finished before he arrived. He was thrown straight into the test, totally unprepared. He did, however, finish top in the navigation selection and was sent to Navigation training school. During his training period Freddy spent his leave periods at home but mostly visiting Nurse Pallister. She was always interested in his progress through his life. Having qualified he was sent on his first posting and after extensive operational experience the story begins.

Freddy was posted and allocated to the flight crew that included 'Pinky' James. The only commissioned officer on board was a Flying Officer Radio Operator who was more inexperienced than any other crew member. He had led a very sheltered life and was completely out of place and treated as a junior member of the crew. He did, however, own an MG sports car which was very useful for evening excursions for the crew. Pinky James was the highly respected crew leader as he was a decorated and very experienced master pilot. He had distinguished himself during the second world war with a large number of confirmed kills.

Although Pinky was a great deal older Freddy and he hit it off straight away and developed a friendship that took them visiting many of the district watering holes in the MG. Flying Officer Peebles was a welcome chauffeur. The story begins when they were transferred to lead an operation which was as the supply squadron to overseas forces posted to Germany and it became a once a week, one day return, flight. The type of aircraft was a great disappointment to Pinky but the fact that it was a weekly trip abroad cheered him. The chance to partake of cheaper 'grog' made Pinky very sensitive to the Varsity aircraft faults on landing and therefore had all checks made to the aircraft before returning to base. The Varsity plane was known as the 'Flying Pig', and from its' appearance and handling it was easy to see why. The number of faults, strangely occurring, always, of course, meant an overnight stay and a night in the sergeants' mess bar.

It became a routine and on one such occasion they arrived in the mess bar. "You threw the kite down today Pinky, is there a problem?" "I needed to do something to wake you up." said Pinky. "It's a wonder you Navigators find the right country never mind the right ruddy airfield." "And God bless you too." said Freddy. "You are welcome," said Pinky "I am getting bored out of my skull with this milk run, it always seems to pour with rain whenever we land in Germany Why can't we get something more exciting, it's not as if the crew lack experience and there are lots of things going on all over the world, a little bit of active service would help."

As they sat in the following silence two very attractive ladies came into the mess. Freddy had seen them before and he had wondered how they gained entry to the Mess unaccompanied. He imagined that the explanation was that the Mess Steward allowed them in to boost the takings. The bar was almost empty but the girls headed straight for them and asked if they could join them. "Of course," said Freddy "be our guests. Can we buy you a drink?" The girls both ordered the same gin and black after introducing themselves as Olga and Heidi. Olga was in her early twenties and she was a very attractive brunette. Her English was perfect and if one did not know any better was English and not German. Heidi was about the same age but she had a heavy accent and was far more reserved than Olga.

Olga sat close to Freddy whilst Heidi sat next to Pinky. Olga and Heidi told the boys that they had both been married but were now single again. No further information was given but Olga said that she had lived in London for many years before returning to her parents' home close to the airfield. "I am alwaya interested in what is happening in England" She said. After a couple more drinks Olga said that she needed some air and asked Freddy to walk with her for a while. They went out through the accommodation entrance and Olga turned and led Freddy to the alcove next to the entrance. The alcove at one time had had a monument or statue housed there but it was now just a large semi-circular, dark inlet. She pulled him closer to her and her arms wrapped around his neck drawing his lips into a demanding kiss. Her passionate sexual advances were just too much to resist and Freddy went along with her sexual demands. Freddy was taken by surprise but he did not resist as it had been some time since he had been on leave. She broke away, after the completed act, just as suddenly as she had started and she smoothed her dress and turned towards the door. She paused and looked back at Freddy just standing, watching her walk away. "I'll get the drinks in." she said and she walked into the bar.

Freddy adjusted his clothing and stood a while wondering what and why? He had never encountered anything like it but he was not complaining. He returned to the bar and Olga. She smiled at him and took a drink of her recently filled gin and black. They sat in a comfortable silence until the door of the Mess diner opened and Pinky emerged with Heidi. Obviously from the smile on his face, Pinky had experienced a similar time with Heidi. Heidi stopped to talk to the young barman before returning to the table. The girls quickly drank their drinks, thanking the boys as they left the Mess and said that they looked forward to the next time.

Freddy and Pinky looked at each other. "What an earth happened there? How did that happen? I've never had anything so matter of fact happen before. Olga did not seem to consider me at all. I think that I have just been taken advantage of, which was novel. I think that things may have taken a turn for the better if they are looking forward to seeing us, we'll have to come back here again. The mess was now deserted except for the boys. "The barman is trying to attract your attention. Have you paid your bar bill?" "Of course I have, I wonder what that 'wallah' wants. I'll go and find out. You are right, I have never known anything like those two girls. Don't let anyone touch my drink." With that Pinky made his way to the bar and was in an intense conversation for some time before he returned. Freddy sat alone with his drink and mulled over the thoughts about what they were doing. It did seem an awful waste of resources flying the Varsity for just one day a week, even though they regularly extended their operation time.

"What seems to be the problem Pinky?" Pinky took a deep drink, almost emptying a full lager glass of mainly gin combined with a splash of tonic. "He must have upset you for you destroy a drink like that, what is it?" Pinky took a deep breath, "He has just offered me all the fags and booze that I can manage for sale in Blighty. The price that he wants is 2d for a packet of Senior Service and a shilling for a bottle of Black Label whisky." "I don't believe it. We could make a fortune at those prices. Is it legal?" "Of course not but I told him that we would talk to him next week and let him know. It means getting the stuff through Marham Customs and unloading without attracting attention back at base. We will have to look into developing a viable M.O. Think about it." "Where's he getting them from at those prices?" asked Freddy. "Best not to ask, let him deal with this end, we have enough on our hands with the logistics of distribution."

They stayed in the Sergeants mess until bedtime and any opportunity or thought of visiting the local town of Wildenrath was dampened by the weather. Following an uneventful return flight, the week dragged on until next Tuesday sortie to Germany. They had made discrete inquiries about demand for drink and cigarettes and they had found much interest and request for cheap supplies. "I've made all necessary arrangements but if you don't want to go ahead with this I will call the whole thing off." said Pinky. "It is more than difficult to ignore the possibilities and the risks are not too bad, I'm sure that we can pull it off as long as we do not take too much each trip. We'll give it just one go and see what happens eh?" "Good lad, I've had a chat with a former associate at Marham and I don't see us having too much to worry about, operation 'Drag 'n' drink' is underway." said Pinky.

# **<u>Chapter 3</u>**

As soon as they arrived in the mess in Germany, Pinky contacted Carl, the young barman, and told him that it was a go. Carl was about twenty something years old. He looked like a real country sort of boy but he was always enthusiastic and friendly to the Mess members. He was married with two daughters and lived locally near the R.A.F. station. He did not seem to be the type to organise and arrange such an operation but Carl said that he would the arrange loading after the bar closed later that night and Pinky said that they would meet him at 0030 hours to oversee everything and make sure that they had only what was needed. The boys spent the rest of the evening in the mess and as usual the girls arrived to entertain the boys…

It was a regular date for the boys now and they looked forward to their visits to the mess. The girls left early as usual but the boys stayed until the bar shut and then they went off to find their aircraft. Freddy and Pinky arrived just after midnight and the aircraft was already taking on its' cargo.

They both wondered how they got access to the plane when it was in the security area. Young Carl seemed to be very well connected. They boarded the aircraft to find that the fuselage was packed with an amazing amount of cigarettes and the flooring on the flight deck had been removed and packed with boxed bottles of black label whisky.

It was after 0200 hours before the flooring and fuselage panels had been replaced and on visual inspection nothing was unusual. The boys expressed concern over the excessive amount that had been loaded but Carl said that they need not pay for it until they sold it all back home. The boys thought that there was far too much but as they had planned a storage area at base which could take it all at a push, they did not make an issue of it. There was no paperwork for any of it and therefore they were not too upset about it.

Flight time was 0800 hours and after very little sleep the boys boarded and the aircraft took to the skies. They soon reached a height to leave the heavily clouded skies behind them and they flew over a mass of white fluffy cloud, it looked like a snow covered landscape and solid enough to land on. During the war time there were fighter pilots who were so battle fatigued that they had perished trying to land on the clouds. The countryside below was totally covered until they reached the North Sea and they could see small fluffy clouds over a sparkling blue sea. Pinky was hoping that customs officer Jones was on duty at Marham but they were concerned and had a 'sweat on' all the way home. Freddy was even more disturbed at the rate of the fuel consumption. "How much extra weight are we carrying? We'll be flying on vapours soon." "Don't panic" said Pinky "we are about to coast in and we'll get some extra aviation fuel to get us back to base at Marham, I'm sure that officer Jones will help us."

"Anything to declare?" asked Jonesy. "We have a couple of packets of cigarettes and a couple of bottles of whisky." Pinky replied. Officer Jones looked at the log and gages, "You've used more fuel than usual, did you make any detours?" Freddy thought that the game was up but Pinky replied, "We hit a very strong headwind over France and our ground speed was about walking pace, we didn't think that we were going to make it." "The Met. Office got it wrong again eh? Let me stamp your contraband and we'll get you topped up to get you back to base."

They could not help smiling to each other as they got airborne again on the way back to base. "I told you 'Jonesy' was ok, mind you, I thought that it was going to get a bit awkward for a while but not to worry we are in the money, the lads will fall over themselves to buy at these prices." said Pinky. He had known Jones from years ago and he was always a little bit different from others on the course which is probably why he did not 'pass out' and failing the course. There was something again that was different about him when Jones did his inspection but Pinky could not really put his finger on what it was.

Carl was absolutely right in that the stock went in just a few hours and the orders flooded in for the next delivery. The future was looking up and over the next few months they had made more money than they had ever done before. Their bank accounts were very healthy and the weekly supply sorties and visits with Heidi and Olga became a regular event and as Christmas approached demand went through the roof.

They looked forward to their visits to Germany but it was without warning that at that time that they hit their first problem. Loading was going well at the German airbase as usual and extra fuel was a standard procedure after the scare at Marham, "You will have a passenger with you this trip." said Carl. "What do you mean? You know that we are not allowed to carry passengers on service trips," said Pinky. "But you must!" said Carl. Carl looked very fearful and after a long pause the boys started to object but from out of the shadows a man suddenly appeared.

Carl physically reacted and stepped back to give a clear view of the intruder. He was a civilian of middle-eastern origin. He was a very large man and from his attitude he was not used to any argument. He was very reminscent of the architypal american gangster villainsof the film industry. He was wearing a wide pin stripe suit and two coloured patent shoes and a large brimmed hat. A heavy black woolen coat was draped across his shoulders. "You have no choice in this matter, you are involved too deeply to have any qualms about such a small request. You will do as we ask without any unpleasantness." The abject fear on Carl's face sent a stark message to the boys and they looked at each other. Pinky was most concerned by Carl's reactions and knew that there was more to this than was immediately apparent.

A period of threatening silence followed, during which time the boys tried to weigh up the situation. It was broken when Pinky realised that the intruder was armed. "Well I suppose that we could go along with it this time," said Pinky. He also realised that this was the thin end of the wedge and that they would be asked to do more and more and he resolved that this was the last trip to Germany on this supply run. Suddenly everything became clear, the cigarettes, the booze, Heidi and Olga, they had fallen into a honey trap and that this man who threatened them was obviously part of a larger powerful organisation. It suddenly became apparent how Carl had been able to set it all up with the boys. He would request the transfer for himself and his crew as soon as he got back, irrespective of the money that they would be giving up but this was just too serious to get involved any further. Both of the boys had seen the tell tale sign of a gun under that jacket of the stranger and although Freddy was ready to object, he bit his tongue and nodded his agreement to Pinky. "Very wise, we would not like to see you come to any harm over such a trivial matter," said the stranger. Carl audibly showed his relief at their consent and a sickly smile appeared on his face, "Can we complete the loading boss?" he asked. "Get on with it!" was the sharp reply and after a long stare at the boys the man quickly faded back into the shadows.

The rest of the crew were not present at this encounter and so they were totally unaware of any of the events involving the stock transfers and were a little puzzled by the conversation on the return flight. The crew was aware that the boys had hit a lucky streak as they had profited along with the boys but they could not help overhearing their conversation as the boys discussed with whom they had become involved', it was obvious that Carl was just a minion and the girls just an encouragement.

# <u>Chapter 4</u>

Pinky was in the Wing Commanders office the first thing the next morning. Wing Commander Fotheringhall was a short and slightly fat individual and he was known to be petty and spiteful. He was not at all respected and he was mostly avoided by aircrew members. How he was ever promoted to his post was a mystery to all who knew him. It was the general belief that the man was so incompetent that station commanders had been pleased to move him on and up. "What is it James?" asked the Wing Commander. "I want to request my crew and I be transferred to another operations section Sir." "Out of the question Master Sergeant, I have specific orders that you are to remain on your present supply runs. These runs are too important to be allocated to an inexperienced replacement crew. We also need to find that so called second navigator that you picked up in Germany on your last trip. I gave no sanction for passengers and to top it all he seems to have gone A.W.O.L. Until this matter is concluded you are going nowhere. Do I make myself clear?" "But Sir" "That is all James." Pinky left his office feeling very confused about the response that he had experienced. How did 'Fothers' know about the passenger? "How did it go?" asked Freddy. "It was very strange, he knew about our passenger and he told me that this supply flight is too important to hand over to another crew." "I don't get it, it's just a routine supply run, any crew could do it," said Freddy "what's so special about this run and how did he know about the passenger and as he does know, why aren't we on a fizzer?" "That's what puzzles me as well," said Pinky, "from the way he was talking I would guess that he knows everything about the flights, including the cargo, why isn't he letting on? We will just have to see what happens on the next run. I have a nasty feeling that it is not just us involved in this project, the information arrived too quickly for it to be coincidental and I don't really understand any of it."

The Tuesday trip without a hitch but as they landed on the return trip at Marham, the aircraft was diverted to a large hanger furthest away from the administration buildings. There was no explanation given but they found themselves directed to a customs office where Officer Jones was waiting for them. He sat behind a large desk and they were both seated opposite on chairs at a lower level than Jones facing the window. This was obviously designed to put the boys at a disadvantage. As they sat in the lower chairs facing the silhouette of Jones Pinky demanded "What's this all about Jones?"

Jones rose from his seat and bent down to lift a case of whisky onto the desk. The boys recognised the case as one of those loaded in Germany. Without a word, Jones ripped open the case and took out a plastic bag of white powder. "Drugs!" said Jones "You have been making waves boys and we do not appreciate you causing any problems for us. Ali warned you in Germany to get on with it without any sort of objection but you went to see your Wing Commander requesting a transfer. You are working for us and you do nothing unless we say so." The boys immediately realised why it had been so easy for them to bring in the cigarettes and whisky.

It became clear to Pinky the difference in Jones' attitude spotted on their last trip. Not only was Jones involved but so was the Wing Commander and goodness knows who else. "How many of these cases have we brought in?" asked Pinky. "You have made plenty from your contraband goods but this is our little perk." said Jones. "You are all in on it and who else is with you?" asked Pinky and Jones replied, "It took you long enough to realise that but you don't have any idea how big or powerful our organisation is and it is now not for you to question. You will do exactly what you are told to do from now on, cross us and you will find yourselves shipped in boxes and dropped in a very deep hole. Your load will be dropped here this time and you will be transported back to your base by truck to pick up your gear. Is that absolutely clear? Your Germany routine is at an end, you will be brought back here for your next flight. Do not attempt to speak to anyone but if they speak to you, you can tell them that you are on special duties. Do you understand?"

The boys nodded and then they were led out to a truck that was already loaded with their cargo. They climbed aboard and as they passed the guard room, the M.P.'s told them that they would see them soon, which was puzzling. They travelled back to base in complete silence but both were wondering what had happened to them over the last few months and they were both increasingly concerned about what the future held for them. It was obvious that they had been lured into a trap and the extent of that trap was now beginning to unfold.

As they drove up to their home base, they were stopped by the guards at the main gate and told to get out of the truck. As they climbed down they were greeted by a smirking Wing Commander

Fotheringhall "Your transport will take you to your new quarters." and he pointed to a large black car. The boys' kit bags were being loaded into the boot. "You will enjoy your new posting seeing as you made the request." said the smirking Wing Commander and he turned and walked away. The boys regarded the Wing Commander with total contempt and anger knowing that he was an intricate part in their situation. The guards moved towards the boys and they were told to get into the car. The door was slammed shut and locked from the front seat of the car.

They were quickly driven away, escorted by a couple of motorcycle outriders. They had not been driving very long before the boys realised that they were heading straight back the way that they had come. The car left the Marham road as the car approached Upper Marham, turning off onto Burnthouse Drove Road and finally into Lady's Wood. Pinky recognised their immediate surroundings but had never been into the wood area. He looked at Freddy with apprehension and Freddy understood his disquiet. The car came to a halt outside of a long and high wall. The wall stretched as far as the boys could see while they sat in the car. On the opposite side of the road was a line of tall trees.

The driver got out of the car without speaking to them and joined one of the outriders on his motor bike. They rode off and were quickly out of sight. The boys sat alone in the car totally nonplussed and they wondered what was going to happen to them. They both thought of making a run for it but they thought that they were still locked in. Had they been able to get out they would not get far carrying their kit bags and they would not like to leave them. Suddenly the passenger door was opened by a middle aged man. "Come on boys, get your gear and follow me. The man did not appear to be in the least bit like the aggressive guards and they felt a bit relieved that their fears may not be as expected. You can leave the car where it is, it will be taken care of."

The man headed for a large gate in the wall which swung open with very little effort and he headed for a very large house which was at the other side of a large quadrangle. "Come on lads!" said the man and the boys followed under the weight of their kit bags. Although the light was not good they could see a manor house that had previously been the hub of a very large estate. The quadrangle was lined by buildings that looked like they had been developed for accommodation, including servant quarters and the lines of stables,

31

some of which had been converted for other purposes but were instantly recognizable by the horse shoes above the doors, confirming their original purpose. There was a row of closed garages with large double doors but the gravelled area did not show any signs of recent activity. Grasses and other plants were gradually taking over the gravelled quadrangle.

The man led them across the quadrangle towards a wing of the manor house, through an open door and up some uncarpeted stairs. They were led to the top floor in the wing of the manor house where there were a number of self contained flats. "This apparently is your posting for the time being, take any of the furnished flats here, whichever you want as there are no other residents at the moment. Breakfast is at 0630 hours. Young Tom will give you a morning call and show you the way to the kitchen." The man went downstairs leaving Freddy and Pinky to explore. They did a quick tour of the rooms. Large rooms had been divided into smaller areas and furnished for one or two people to occupy. All the rooms seemed to be approximately designed from a standard plan and were very basic but comfortable. Looking out of the windows they could see the rear gardens which were unkept but extensive. Lawns spread from the house with trees interspersed to give separate areas. They could a large expanse of woods in the distance.

Looking to the front they could see the quadrangle where they had arrived and woods over the high wall. They chose the two larger adjacent rooms closest to the staircase, dumped their kit bags and fell into bed.

# <u>Chapter 5</u>

The boys both felt that they had just closed their eyes when Tom banged on their doors waking them for breakfast. Tom was a young, fresh faced lad and though he did not talk much he seemed quite pleasant. He waited for them to wash and dress and then led them down a stair case that had once been used by staff. The staircase led straight into a large kitchen on the ground floor. The kitchen was large with an open stove that would take a whole hog on a spit. The irons were still in place. The stove had ovens heated by the fire in which food could be kept warm or cooked. There were a number of doors leading out of the kitchen, one of which led to the servants' quarters. That was the door that they had used. It was obvious that this had been a very important and very well staffed private estate at one time.

They sat at a large wooden table where a cook of days long gone would have prepared giant meals for those upstairs. They enjoyed a very hearty breakfast but as they ate, confused thoughts made it difficult to understand what had happened to them and what plans were in store for them. Why they were where they were made no sense to them whatsoever. They sat quietly drinking a cup of tea when the kitchen door opened to reveal the man from the shadows in Germany. He entered the kitchen. The boys just could not believe that this man was here in England. In the daylight they were confronted by a very large man.

He reminded Freddy of a Greek wrestler. He had a fleshy face but his appearance was that of a man of a very cruel nature. His mouth twisted as he spoke which made the sickly smile on his face quite grotesque. "My name is Ali Ishmail and I control all operations in this part of the world. You will no doubt have many questions but let me explain, you two no longer exist. All record of your existence has been erased from every record everywhere in the world. The rest of your crew have been split up and posted separately. You have been chosen to work for us. You will be given orders that will be obeyed without question. You will be given a few days to familiarise yourselves with our private aircraft and you will be operational in three days time. Failure to comply will be fatal and failure is not an option. Is that perfectly clear? You now belong to us and you will do as you are told without question." The boys nodded in dismay. Ali turned and left the kitchen.

Freddy was first to break the silence, "This has

to be some sick kind of joke. They can't get away with this kind of stuff in England." Pinky replied, "It looks as if they can do it and they have done it but the question is who are these people and what do they want with us? They must carry some clout if Ali is right. We must have become involved with a very powerful organization if they can wipe our service records, they must have control in some very high places. Do they belong to our security set up or some other? How can they wipe out our existence in records? We will just have to go along with it until we see how the land lies and what they have in mind for us."

At that, the door opened and Tom and the older man came in. "I am sorry that I could not introduce myself earlier but I was under instructions and they are not the sort of people that I would like to upset. My name is Alan and I own this place. We normally have groups staying with us but it is a quiet period at the moment and they have paid to hire the whole place so who am I to argue? They say that you will only be here for a short time, I'm not sure how long and they tell me that they will come for you by car when you are needed. You have the freedom of the manor but I have to warn you not to try to leave, they tell me that the consequences will not be pleasant, whatever that means. Tom and I will help you but we know nothing other than you are to stay with us a while, anything outside of that and we cannot help. They say that they are a Government Department but we don't really know who these people are. They have just paid well for your accommodation but we have been told not to discuss anything that we see with you. It's a funny goings on but business is business. The pantry is well stocked and so is the bar next door. Help yourselves to anything that there is and you have the complete run of the place. Have a pleasant few days boys." Alan left them with Tom.

"What can you tell us about this Tom?" said Freddy "and who is this guy Ali?" "You heard what Alan said but I've never seen that fellow before, he is one of Alan's customers. I have heard Alan on the phone to him once or twice but Alan said that he would pay very good money to look after two men coming to visit for a few days. I was told to show you around and help you find what you wanted." "What does Alan do? I mean does he work?" asked Freddy. "I've never known Alan have a job, if that's what you mean.

I came here when I was very young, a baby in fact and I have never known my parents but Alan and his wife always have looked after me. The wife died years some ago from some illness. I was never told what illness. They have never been short of money so I think that they must have investments or something. I will have to go now I have some jobs to do, see you in a while crocodile." "Well that wasn't much help was it but we do know that they are not part of whatever the plan is." said Pinky. "I don't like this at all and there is nothing we can do about it for a while, so I suppose that we will just have to sit tight, I just wish that I could get my hands on that Wing Commander." said Freddy. Pinky nodded his agreement.

The events of the next two days consisted of trips in the car to the Marham airfield and familiarisation with an aircraft that Pinky thought was Russian made but had English labelling on the instruments. It was quite alien to Pinky and it took quite a few hours to become familiar with all the controls. The navigation system was also new to Freddy who had never seen such a radar/radio communication system. The only vague comparison that they could make was to a DC3. All other times were spent back at the manor house where they saw very little of anyone else.

The manor was bigger than they had first thought and the grounds beyond the building were varied and extensive. Freddy walked alone through the grounds lost in his own little world. As he walked he tried to imagine the estate in its' former glory. There must have been a considerable number of staff to keep the place going. From the portraits in the house he imagined a well to do family walking the grounds, the ladies in long flowing dresses and the men in formal dress. The children were of course not allowed to be near the adult family and were probably being looked after by nannies or a house keeper. The grandeur of his thoughts cut out his present predicament for a while and he strolled through the ages in his thoughts. As he approached the manor house he was brought back to reality with a realisation of his and Pinky's situation. After they had had lunch in the kitchen both boys set of together to look around the estate and grounds.

As they walked they were aware that they were being followed at a discreet distance by at least two men. Earlier Freddy had not been aware of any followers but he realised that he must have been observed by somebody. After a while, they forgot about their observers and wandered through the gardens and woods on the estate. They talked about the past events and how they had become involved in something that they could not understand but as they they talked they understood that they had been targeted for some reason and purpose to the benefit of this strange organisation. They were on their guard but could not imagine what lay ahead of them.

They spent the best part of the next day eating and sleeping and though there was every alcoholic drink available to them, neither felt like drinking. On the second evening following, they were sat twiddling their thumbs and they were quite bored when the door burst open and Tom told them to pack their flying bags and be ready to leave early next morning. The kit bags could be left for the time being.

The next morning the boys were washed and dressed when Tom came to tell them that they were to leave in thirty minutes. There was just time to grab a bite to eat before the car came to take them to the airfield. Tom had already put their flying kit in the car while they ate. The boys asked the driver where they were going but they were told that they would find out when they got there. They drove the short distance and entered Marham airfield through a perimeter gate and the aircraft was parked within in hundred yards of the entrance.

# <u>Chapter 6</u>

They boarded and were told to maintain radio silence, no contact with the control tower. They were given local F.I.R. settings and they prepared for take-off in their own time. A now familiar threatening voice told them that the heading was for West Berlin airfield and to maintain radio silence all the way. The F.I.R. details were displayed on the strange radar set and altered as they left each region. They did exactly as Ali told them. They were not alone on the flight-deck, two uniformed, armed guards watched them at all times. They were all on the same intercom so everybody could hear what was said. Only Pinky spoke to Ali saying that there was a Berlin blockade and they might be shot down when entering West Berlin.

The intercommunication system stayed quiet, no response. The boys were unable to talk to each other without being overheard so the flight continued in silence. The flight over the North Sea was quite bumpy but as they coasted into France the weather became perfect flying conditions. The fields and farm houses were clearly in view as they flew over the countryside. They were both getting more unsettled with the situation, especially as they approached the West Berlin airfield. Suddenly the radio/radar system burst into life with landing instructions and the aircraft landed without challenge or approach by any sort of security. On landing Pinky was told to prepare for immediate take-off after refueling. A tanker vehicle quickly linked up with the aircraft and soon completed the job of preparing the aircraft for take-off. They were ready to go when a small group of men ran across the airfield towards them. Pinky was told to wait for them to get on board. As soon as the hatch was closed, the order was given to take-off and head back to Marham. Pinky felt quite silly after he asked over the communication system what customs would make of this but he just felt that he had to say something. His comments were completely ignored and everything went without a hitch back to Marham.

The boys were driven back to the manor house and for the first time on arrival could speak freely. "I knew that we wouldn't be challenged on landing. Whoever or whatever this organization is they must have this place completely under their control." said Pinky. "That occurred to me as well but I also think that I know why we are here. They know that we know nothing about them so if we get caught on this mission, whatever it is, we can't tell anyone anything. I recognised a member of the party that got on board and that really does worry me. The leading runner was Fidel Castro, I would know him anywhere. It was either him or a very close double. I think that we are being used for a suicide mission." replied Freddy. Pinkys' mouth dropped open, "You surely can't be serious. Was that really Castro? Whatever is he doing over here?" "Whatever this  operation is we are expendable and may not make it alive but if we succeed we are definitely done for anyway. That's why our records have been destroyed," said Freddy "I think that we are in the proverbial Pinky." Pinky looked hard at Freddy and thought for a while, "I think that you are right. At least we know what we are up against so we need to be prepared for all eventualities. Watch for any opportunity that presents itself and in the meantime don't let on that you suspect what they are up to. Especially don't let them know that you saw and recognised one of the passengers"

The boys sat around for the next few days, surprised that they were back at the manor house with very little sign of Tom over that time. They had tried to scale the wall to escape but each time they tried anything an armed guard appeared from nowhere. The guards were never in view and their stationing was a very well kept secret. They were never in sight until an attempt to escape occurred. There had to be someone monitoring the gate at all times because each time they got close to it a guard would appear. They thought constantly about escape scenarios but even if they got away what could they do and where would they go without identities? In a world where they knew that officially they no longer existed. As they were having breakfast one morning Tom came and said "You have a night flight tonight, be ready to leave at 1800 hours." He turned and went out leaving the boys astounded at his actions. "That wasn't like Tom at all I've never seen him so agitated. The job must be on tonight, I wonder what they have in store for us?" said Freddy." "Well, Castro must still be around somewhere. They couldn't move him around the countryside without causing a stir of some sort. I wonder if our mission has something to do with him and transport out of the country to goodness knows where." replied Pinky. They both knew that this was crunch time and they had to be aware of any chance of getting away before the inevitable. They had to keep their wits about them, it was now or never. The evening was overcast and it was quite dark but the wind was very light and a slight mist was developing. When the time came to go, two armed men took them by car to Marham airbase and straight to a waiting aircraft. The airfield was covered in slowly swirling mist which made long vision a bit of a lottery. As soon as they got on board Pinky whispered to Freddy that he had flown this very aircraft in nineteen forty six just after the Second World War. It was one of five bought from the American Air Force and this is the one that he had to test fly. Now it was clear why they had been chosen. It was one of the first Constellation flight purchased before the Lockheed 049 fleet were bought. Pinky told Freddy that they must be in for a long journey and that Freddy must be correct in who they had picked up in Berlin. One of the armed men ordered them to be silent and take up their positions. The passengers were boarding and the boys were now certain of their identities. Pinky said "This is it Freddy we have to look for any opportunity now that it is make or break, fingers crossed we get a chance."

The intercommunications burst into life with instructions to take off in ten minutes on a heading of 270 degrees. Freddy put on his helmet and acknowledged. He thought on what Pinky had said and he was in better spirits than he had been in some time. As soon as they were in the air a course was set for due west and they settled down at cruise speed. The mist was quickly left behind as it was very close ground mist and it was clear after just a few feet of climb. They both knew that they were in for a long haul flight and maintaining radio silence as usual. Freddy had to guess what the F.I.R. variations might be, so they continued their flight on direct vision and pure assessment of air pressures and conditions from previous meteorological forecasts. They were given more details of the flight plan as they flew across the Atlantic Ocean. Freddy realized that they were heading for America but was not sure why they were not taking the southern Atlantic crossing. It dawned on him that the Atlantic patrols would question their identity and may prove to become problematic. The northern route took much longer as the prevailing wind was head on and slowing their progress. They changed heading to 330 degrees and after some time landed at an airfield in Canada for refuelling and then set a course due south. As they flew across American air space they were occasionally investigated by military aircraft but they didn't come under any pressure from them as they were recognised as an American made aircraft. The outer insignia had not been clear on previous viewing so neither of the boys knew of any recognition marks. They were allowed to fly on unimpeded. They landed twice more for refuelling.

Pinky thought that the final filling wasn't necessary but each time they landed they took on more equipment. Pinky realised that the extra weight was the need to take on more fuel. At last he was informed of the destination and to his amazement he learned that it was San Julian Air Base in Cuba. On landing the extent of the cargo unloaded was far more than either of the boys had imagined. They saw everyone disembark except the two armed guards and Freddy tried the flight deck door "We are still locked in here." At that the door opened and one of the guards ordered them to take off straight away on a heading of 310 degrees. The door was closed as the guard left but noticeably not locked. The aircraft took off on the prescribed heading. The intercom. had been silent even before take-off, which was unusual, so after thinking about it for a few minutes Pinky set the auto pilot as he was aware that they were heading back into American air space. Pinky ventured through the unlocked door and disappeared for a while only to return very excited "There is no one on board except us. I've checked everywhere." "Great then let's take this baby home." said Freddy. Pinky took the controls and tried to manoeuvre but the controls had been remotely locked by a timing device. They were coasting in to mainland America heading in a direction for Oklahoma or Kansas. "I have no control, the auto pilot will not turn off and I can't do a thing about it. I have no idea how they have jammed all the controls." exclaimed Pinky. Pinky carried on "By the time I find out what it is that they have done we will have run out of fuel and headed for the deck." They both abandoned their positions and searched the aircraft looking for parachutes but all they found was a load of papers in a hold-all. They thought that were completely trapped when it occurred to Pinky "We always kept spare chutes under your navigation position when I flew this crate last. Freddy go and see if you can still find them." Freddy returned a little later wearing a parachute and he handed another to Pinky who quickly put it on. "All this paperwork is in Russian and it looks as if we have become traitors helping this lot. I will keep this stuff for future use because it might be helpful to prove that we are not spies." Pinky stuffed the paperwork and two large envelopes into his flying suit having checked one and found some American Bonds in there. He hoped that they might be as good as cash if and when they were needed. They went to open the doors to escape but found all of the exits had been sealed shut. They were trapped. It occurred to Pinky that the navigation loading bay door might have been overlooked and so they set off back to the flight deck and dropped into the navigation bay door space. This door also seemed to be sealed. They sat there in despair for a few minutes and they were chilled to hear the aircraft engine noise change. "We must be flying on vapours." said Pinky and in pure frustration he kicked out at the navigation bay door which burst open taking the boys by surprise. The boys found themselves in space falling out from beneath the navigation position. The doors had burst open and they had fallen out under the aircraft. They deployed their parachutes as quickly as they could which was a mistake as they were above ten thousand feet and without oxygen and they both felt quite light headed in such low oxygen levels. Their breathing soon returned to normal as they descended and their spirits rose at their unexpected freedom. They descended through sun warmed space in a very light breeze. They started to enjoy the descent and the view of the landscape below and the large town which was not too far from where they would land. They were shocked out of their thoughts by a loud explosion and they saw bits of the Constellation and black smoke drifting towards the earth. They both realised that they had just made it out of the aircraft in time. Ali and friends had taken every conceivable opportunity to make sure that the boys did not survive. As they drifted to the ground Freddy took notice of the area below them. They were heading very close to a road below that appeared to head for a very large town to the west of their position. Before the road reached the town there was a small village on the same road. They both came to ground safely and quickly disposed of their parachutes, hiding them well out of sight in a wooded area. Freddy said, "We need to get out of our flying suits, we would be very conspicuous in them. We have shirt and trousers that will more fit the bill in this part of the U.S.A." Remembering the direction of the large town seen from the air they soon made it to a highway and headed towards town. As they walked they discussed their lucky escape and wondered if they would be thought of as now dead by their captors. They concluded that that would be the best outcome as long as they could stay undetected by any of the authorities. They had been walking for quite a while when an old truck approached from behind them. Freddy thumbed a list and to their relief the truck came to a halt beside them. "Howdy boys you headed for town?" came the question from the driver. "We are aiming for the town up the road." The driver told them to jump up onto the back of the truck. They thanked the driver and climbed aboard. As they were travelling Pinky had  a good look at the bonds in the envelope from the aircraft and was astounded to find about fifty, ten thousand American dollar bonds, "We will have to risk trying to cash one or two of these bonds. We haven't any money on us and we can't get very far without some collateral. If there is a Bank of America in Dallas, we will try there'. They had just passed a road sign directing them to Dallas which showed that Pinky's navigation skills were not what he imagined. They passed through the small hamlet which was called Kaufman and soon arrived in the outskirts of Dallas. The driver with a goodbye wave let them get out of the truck in the banking district which was a very welcome and an unexpected coincidence. It did not take long to find a Bank of America and they offered one of the bonds to the cashier. After a long look at them and the bond, the cashier handed over the cash without further question. As soon as they left the bank they divided the money so that were both independent and could manage if they were separated. They agreed that they would need transport as a priority and headed for a car dealer that  they passed on the road as they got to the banking district. They walked along the road towards the car dealer's place but the Dallas that they had seen on TV and films was nothing like what they now experienced. They passed crowds of Americans but nobody gave them a second glance and they soon began to relax and felt that maybe their ordeal was at last over. For just a couple of hundred dollars they drove away from the garage with a full tank of petrol in a nearly new Chevrolet convertible. Freddy said "We need to get as far away from here as fast as we can. We need as much distance between the wreckage of that aircraft and us as we can get. It is sure to be reported on the radio and people just might connect us as strangers to the event. What is the best direction for us to take?" Pinky replied "I worked with a young American pilot on the aircraft transfers in 1946 and he lived and worked in Washington D.C. so I think that that is our best bet. I am sure that he will remember me and I am sure that he will help us to get out of this mess." They headed on route thirty towards Arkansas and onto route sixty-six. Freddy was fairly familiar with American maps and knew that once on route sixty-six Washington signs were easy to follow. "I'm glad that you know where you are going, I wouldn't have a clue." said Pinky remembering his previous destination estimate. They shared the driving knowing that it would take hours and hours to reach Washington especially as they would need to stop for a rest somewhere on route. It had been many hours since they had had any sleep and night flights do take a toll on concentration. They were both getting very tired and they had frequent stops to avoid falling asleep and to stretch their legs. In consequence it took far longer than it should have done to reach Texarkana where they stopped and booked a couple of rooms at a motel on west 9th street. It was a rundown boarding house rather than a motel but the owners made an effort to keep the place clean and tidy. The sheets were fresh and clean and felt so welcome after their journeys. They fell asleep as soon as they lay down on their beds. They had booked a morning call but they were both up and dressed before the call came. The owner was very inquisitive about two 'limies' staying at his place but they said that they were just touring. After a hearty breakfast they made enquiries about the nearest Bank of America and were outside the bank as the door opened. The owner had been very insistent on the boys talking about themselves and how they had acquired Bank America accounts. They hastened off to the bank as soon as they could get away. Without any problem they each cashed two bonds and left the bank. Once outside they got into the Chevrolet and headed on route sixty six to Arkansas. The journey was very pleasant, Freddy had not travelled the roads of America before and he found that it was quite relaxing compared with U.K travel. They made it to Little Rock, Arkansas in good time and went straight to the bank and cashed another two bonds each. The bank clerk looked at them in an inquiring way but did not hesitate in cashing the bonds. They now had plenty of money in case of any emergencies that might occur.

They decided to take a break and spent the afternoon and evening taking in the sights of the city which relaxed them before bed. They came across the Arkansas Arts Center located on the corner of 9th and Commerce streets in MacArthur Park, there was lots of activity and a lot of development work was going on. One of the people watching struck up a conversation with the boys. He was very interested in their accents and where they came from. He thought that he had ancestors in the U.K. and wondered if they knew of his family, the Browns, who he thought lived near London, England. The boys told him that they lived a lot further north and could not help. Jed had been born in Little Rock and was proud to explain that the Mayor was leading a group of developers upgrading and expanding the Arts Centre. They thanked Jed and set off to explore further. As they walked they wondered if they had been wise telling Jed about themselves but decided that he seemed genuine enough and they stopped worrying about their meeting.

The next morning, they left Little Rock, Arkansas and headed on to the next big town but when they tried to cash more bonds they met a problem. The cashier was presented with the bonds but he headed for the back office only to return with a blank refusal to pay out. He asked them to accompany him to the office. The boys demanded the return of the bonds and promptly left. They realised that the banks had been alerted and they left town as quickly as possible aware now that their previous captors knew that they had somehow escaped their trap and were still alive. How they had got the information to the bank and its' staff amazed them. They hit the road again and headed non-stop for Washington D.C. After some consideration they concluded that; "It was obvious really that if we kept drawing money it would soon register with their organisation that we had the bonds from the aircraft." said Pinky. "We had no choice Pinky," said Freddy "They are not stupid these people, whoever they are and they must keep account of their finances. They would soon realise that we or someone else was cashing the bonds left on the Constellation, in fact, they knew that if we survived it was likely that we would find them and spend them.  In fact, it might have been a follow up trap. They will now know our heading by the trail that we left. We need to get any help from your friend as quickly as possible. They might already be on our tails." The journey was taking more time than they had accounted for and the distances were greater than first thought. They continued their journey, sleeping alternately as the other drove the car.

Back in England Charlie King addressed the airmen gathered together in Hilary's cafe, Aunt Sally's in Bedale.  It  was the best eater near the air bases  where they were all based. "Look lads, we have waited long enough for Freddy and Pinky to get here for this reunion.  Does anybody know where they have been posted? I sent invitations to our last base and asked them to post them on.  I can't see any of our old crew missing out on a reunion. Yvonne, have you seen any of the boys lately?" Yvonne replied that she hadn't seen anyone since the last meeting at the cafe.  Jack the radio operator said "I tried to contact them through records but it was very strange because they said that they had no records of either of them.  I couldn't find any trace of them being on operations with us either which is crazy." Charlie looked around the group, they were all very quiet. "Has no one heard from them?" There was no response. "Well lads, something is very wrong here has anyone asked around?" Roger said that he had been in touch with his very good friend, Jane in administration and she said that she would get back to him with any news of Freddy or Pinky. She had not been in touch at all. When he had phoned back to ask her again someone else answered and when he asked for Jane he was told that he must be mistaken, there was no Jane in admin. "What the hell is going on here?" said Charlie "look lads we need to get to the bottom of this. Cubby you have a high up relation in the M.O.D. can you contact him and make some discreet enquiries? The rest of you find out what you can and we will meet back here next week at the same time. I don't like the sound of all this so be as discreet as you can and do everything that you can lads." Before he left he spoke to Hilary and told her how worried they all were and checking that she was happy about them having the upstairs room next week.

Cubby got a weekend pass as soon as he got back and took the first available train to London. He had contacted his cousin who held a high office in the Ministry of Defense and arranged to stay with him over the next two days. He arrived at King's Cross and he took the Green Line underground train to Gloucester Road station. He arrived at Petersham Place late in the evening to be greeted by his cousin Godfrey Bellinger. Petersham Place was a select location not far from Kensington Palace. The white painted houses were very expensive to upkeep but they were most sort after by those who could afford. The interior was very sparsely furnished and decorated but it contained all the essentials that a bachelor would need. Cubby was quite surprised how Spartan Godfrey lived but he sipped his gin and tonic and chatted to Godfrey about all the latest family news. Godfrey appeared to be very interested as he had very little contact with any of the family members. Godfrey worked in circles that were familiar to him but far removed from the normal life of the family. "Well old chap," said Godfrey "I'm sure that you didn't travel all this way just to chat about Aunty Elaine and the rest, what's the problem?" Cubby told him about the crew and the reunion and the fact that Freddy and Pinky had completely disappeared. He told him about their enquiries being blocked, stonewalled and being told that people they know had never worked at places where they had recently been contacted. "Goodness gracious," exclaimed

Godfrey "if what you say is true then it would appear that we have one almighty security problem. From what you say, I wonder who can we trust? There appears to be some corruption in your services. We will have a look and see what we can find out. We need to find your chaps without delay and gather all the information that we can. Leave it with me. My friend in security will know exactly what to do." Cubby was startled when Godfrey jumped up and said that he was off to see his security chap. He appeared not deterred by the fact that it was Friday evening and much of the ministry would be empty. Godfrey left the house at Petersham Place and headed for the ministry office, having informed Sir George Curswell that he was on his way. Cubby was left at Godfrey's house with instructions to stay as long as he wished so he went for a discovery tour of the house and then settled down for a relaxing evening with access to Godfrey's bar.

Sir George was waiting in his office for Godfrey to arrive, "What's the flap Godfrey? I am not very happy about having my Friday night interrupted. I do hope that it is something important that you have to report." "We may have a major security breach on our hands old chap."

Godfrey went on to explain what had happened and how Cubby had come to see him with his story. "My goodness we can't have chaps disappearing without trace or record. Are you sure that this is not some kind of prank?" replied Sir George. "Cubby is a very reliable young man and I wouldn't doubt that he was deadly serious but it can't be too serious, it may just be down to forces records." said Godfrey. Sir George sat silent for a few minutes and looked very serious. "This is just incredible. I have been working through  the implications of what you have described, we must find these chaps. The corruption must be extensive in more than one of our government departments. service records haven't got the power to mess with data. Who can we trust? Leave this with me overnight. I will meet you at nine tomorrow morning at the usual Green Park rendezvous." Godfrey was now questioning if it was wise to involve Sir George, it might blow up into something serious. Godfrey decided to stay over in town at the Union Club at St' James for the night so that he would be close to the mornings rendezvous. He was a club member and the rooms were very comfortable and the food was excellent. He spent the evening dining and chatting in the bar lounge where service was very attentive. Godfrey arrived early next morning but saw Sir George already waiting for him. "At last Godfrey," as if he was surgesting that he was late, "I conducted a little investigation of my own last night and your cousin was correct. I could not find any record of the chaps that you mentioned. It looks as if we will have to be very careful who we trust in command in the services and in the ministry departments. We need an independent operative who knows his onions. We need someone who is anonymous. We have used a trusted agent on previous occasions called Huntley Haverstock. Very rew people would know him. We always contact him through the Times advertising. We can't be seen to be involved in any investigation as it may alert whoever is behind all this. I will appoint Huntley and get him to contact you at the Petersham house and you will liaise directly with me, if that is alright with you? You will have to inform your guest that you have taken steps to find out what's

happened and you will keep him in the picture" Godfrey nodded and they parted. As Godfrey travelled back to his house, he felt that he had opened a can of worms that would disturb his comfortable life style and arrived home feeling quite disturbed. Sir George went back to his office and contacted the Sunday Times to insert an advertisement for Huntley under the Harley

Davison code contact. He checked the file on Huntley and he was reassured that he had chosen well.

In the North East of England in a local rugby club, Tony Grey was enjoying lunch with his wife Rosemary when Barney came to their table. "Hey Tony, this is right up your street. You answered one of these advertisements about a Harley Davison bike before but you didn't get one. There is another special Harley for sale here." Barney handed the paper to Tony. Tony got up and with Rosemary they left straight away, leaving Barney wondering what he had said. Tony contacted the advertisement telephone number saying that he was interested in the Harley Davison background chart. The code was immediately recognised by Sir George "Is that you Huntley?" Tony confirmed giving the code response. "You are needed at once at the Petersham house without delay." The telephone line went quiet and the call was ended.

Huntley Haverstock arrived early Monday morning at Petersham Place. He dismounted from his Ducati motorcycle and parked it outside Godfrey's house. He didn't remove his helmet after ringing the doorbell. Codes were exchanged and Huntley was invited into the house. Godfrey didn't speak but handed Huntley a package and a letter of introduction to the Union Club in St. James. Nothing further was said and Huntley left and headed for the St. James club. He was shown to a room whilst a footman parked Huntley's Ducati in a secure area. When he settled into his room Huntley read the file containing information and instructions to investigate the disappearance of two airmen. He must conduct the investigation at all times in total secrecy. Money, security I.D. and passes were included in the package. He read the file over and over in complete disbelief at the possible corruption and the possibility that there was foreign infiltration into Government departments and armed forces. Sir George had made extensive enquiries and found that many more departments had been involved in this mystery. After his long journey Huntley decided to take time for a rest and then set off for Marham air base. He turned on the radio to hear the national news broadcast and was shocked to hear that a worldwide crisis was being reported. The newsreader reported that Cuba had begun to install Russian missiles at their air bases and was creating a threat against the U.S.A. No one knew how the missiles arrived there as the U.S.A. military monitored all traffic in and out of Cuba, it was a mystery. American officials were expressing their anger about the threatening Communist presence so close to their shores and there was talk of war. People around the world were talking about four minute warnings and everyone was fearful of another world war. Later that day Huntley set off for Marham. As Huntley was leaving the club he noticed a man sitting in an overcoat in the very well heated Union Club lounge. Huntley was on the alert and as he rode away along Pall Mall. He saw a black Bentley car following and matching his speeds. To check that he was not imagining things he made a quick detour and the Bentley followed. Huntley stopped at a news agents shop and watched as the Bentley kept on going past. He headed out of London on the road to Marham. It came as a shock when he saw the same Bentley car about four hundred yards behind him again matching his speed. He turned into the first café and lorry stop that was familiar to him along the road. He parked the Ducati out of sight at the rear of the cafe and went in through the cafe front door. As he entered the door he saw the Bentley turn in and park. Three of the Bentley occupants followed him into the cafe. Huntley made sure that they heard him order a full English breakfast with a mug of tea. He took his breakfast, which he certainly did not need after the club breakfast and sat down at a table close to the toilet door. He placed the food on the table and sat down. He had a good view of the service counter and the rest of the tables. He discreetly watched as the trio took a table by the front door. After a minute or two Huntley got up and stretched leisurely and leaving his breakfast untouched on the table he strolled into the toilet. Quickly he left the building through the toilet window and started his bike and headed up the farm path at the side of the cafe that he had noticed as he arrived. He had seen a wooded area further up the path and made for it knowing that any followers would have to be on foot. He hid in the woods and it wasn't long before he saw his followers running around looking for him or his bike. They eventually went back to the car and turned in the direction of Marham, assuming that Huntley had resumed his journey. Huntley planned a route away from main the roads, it would take a little longer but it would be much safer. He wondered if his followers were standard surveillance or was his mission already compromised. Huntley remembered his R.A.F. service years in air traffic control and as he approached Marham he considered those who may still be serving here in Customs and air traffic control. He quickly contacted those he had served with and who were still there in both groups and took a risk of carefully questioning those members that he considered most reliable.

Although no one knew anything specific Huntley put together the information and came up with a revealing account of the events of the night Constellation flight and its' aircrew. Having offered his thanks and goodbyes Huntley set off to go straight back to London. On his return journey he took particular care to check for any followers and he arrived back to the Union Club without any further incident. From the club he contacted Godfrey and made arrangements to pass all his information over to him. Godfrey told him to stand by for further instructions and then contacted Sir George and relayed the information to him. Sir George called together his most trusted agents but before the meeting he checked with the Air Traffic Security Team. They had discovered a secret flight that had left the U.K. air space flown by a crew of whom they had been unable to find any record. The crew may not have been willing parties to the flight from information received but the crew need to be found without delay. This looked like a serious security breach and they were waiting for the F.B.I response for possible destinations on the American continent. Sir George addressed his agents giving them the information received from Air Traffic security and he continued, "As soon as I have any more news I will forward it through the usual channels set up for red code one. The crew could be anywhere by now but I want those men found and brought here." The agents dispersed with the knowledge that this was a top priority mission.

The U.S. Secret service was concentrating on the same mission, they had known about an aircraft explosion in American air space but it had not been thought to be significant at the time. The information from British sources changed all that and it was now a top priority. The proximity of the exploding aircraft to Cuban air space rang alarm bells at the Whitehouse. Priority instructions were given to all agencies to find the Constellation crew assuming they were still alive. It was soon confirmed, with all the new information, that an aircraft had left American air space bound for Cuba and on returning, exploded near Dallas Texas. The search and investigation was on.

Freddy and Pinky sat in a motel stunned by the news of the Cuban crisis. They now knew that they had been used in connection with the cause of the crisis but the extent to which they weren't sure as they were not sure what cargo they had carried. They had not been able to contact the friend in

Washington D.C. They had to leave when things became uncomfortable when they asked the whereabouts of the friend. They thought that unnecessary questions about their identities were being made and they suspected that they were being monitored in their enquiries. It was confirmed when they realised that they were being followed by two motorcycle outriders on the highway. They had left the highway as soon as an opportunity to leave the main roads presented itself. The roads were narrow and twisting as they made their way through the American back roads. They were unsure from time to time about their exact position and sometimes they were not certain of their heading. The roads that they were on made their way through tree lined avenues and meandered from south to north on occasions. The terrain changed so quickly from the familiar to the most unfamiliar. They were aware that they were on route 56 but were relieved that at last they knew where they were. They arrived at Middleburg and left the main street where, off the main highway they changed the car and replaced it with a pickup truck and made their way to a small motel on W. Federal Street. As they sat in one of the rooms Pinky exclaimed "How did we let ourselves get involved in all this? I don't know what to do now. They are going to keep on hounding us until they catch us and kill us." The sound of a fast car approaching and then braking rapidly set their nerves on edge. Doors crashed open and loud voices could be heard as if from all directions. The boys froze. There was a tremendous crash as the door next to their room was broken down and shots were fired into the room. They thought that they had been chased to this motel and they feared that it would be their room next. They heard the sound of people running and all went quiet. They sat still, hardly breathing, when a knock came at their door. They thought it better not to open it but the voice of the desk clerk called them by name. Freddy opened the door and was greeted by the white faced clerk who asked if they were okay. He went on to say that two gang members had been gunned down in the room next door after a shoot- out. He was glad to hear that the boys had not been harmed. The gangsters were known to him as they had demanded protection money from the motel takings so he wasn't too upset at the outcome of the incident. The boys were relieved to know that they were innocent bystanders in this incident but they realized that it could very well have been their pursuers after them. Freddy suggested, "We have got to stay off the main roads and keep going. I know of a place in the Catskills near Monticello where no one will find us.

It is up in the state of New York so it is quite a ride to get there but I think we will be quite safe. The place used to be a summer camp for New Yorkers and mainly used by the Jewish children. I was once offered an exchange job there during the school holidays and the reports were very good. We will have to avoid the main highways so it will take us longer to get there but once there we can lay low as long as we need. The guy who used to own it went burst some time ago. We have the money and we can buy enough supplies to stay there indefinitely." "Good idea," said Pinky "if we travel by night and sleep during the day we will have more of a chance of making it." The rest of the day was spent looking around the area. They found a very pleasant eating place called 'Fat Boys' which supplied them with an excellent meal for a very reasonable price. They stayed at the motel until dark and then set off north heading for New York State. It was slow progress on the back roads, twisting and turning back and forth and as they travelled through the night. It was taking them far more time to make progress and they were forced onto the main highway by merging roads but two nights later they made it to route seventeen off route 87 and 6 before it was light. They travelled on and approached Ramsey Motel just before the sun was up. They were physically and mentally exhausted and when they got to their rooms they were asleep in no time and slept until late afternoon. They were wakened by the  sound of heavy vehicles passing the motel. They made enquiries at the desk by phone but the reception could not help, other than to say that it was most unusual to have such traffic. They dismissed the occurrence as possible circus traffic. They had heard that the U.S.A. was keen on small town circuses.  They freshened up  and  left  the motel as the light was fading heading for Monticello and relative safety. The idea of getting there made them feel a little more relaxed and the plan to lay low there gave them a bit more confidence that things would somehow get better. On the smaller roads traffic was very light so they cruised along in good spirits even though it was getting quite dark and overcast. They passed abandoned houses on the forest roads where people had just moved on a little further up the road and built another house. It was quite strange for the boys to understand. It was most unlike any British idea. Suddenly a couple of miles up ahead of them Freddy saw some very bright stationery lights. Freddy asked "Do you think that it is a road block ahead?" Pinky agreed and they decided to turn around and try and find another way to their  destination.  Before they had a chance to turn around they spotted some motorcycle outriders coming up fast behind them, followed by a very fast large vehicle. The riders were very familiar to them and they knew immediately that Ali's men had found them. Just as they spotted their pursuers shots rang out and the rear pickup window glass exploded into thousands of pieces covering them both with shards of glass. Freddy accelerated but they both knew that they could not outrun them. More shots hit the rear of the truck and as they were approaching the road block their attention turned to what was ahead but then there was a loud explosion just behind them. "We've had it," said Freddy "they've got rockets." Fear gripped them both and they knew that there was nowhere for them to turn or avoid their pursuers. Pinky looked to the rear of them and saw that the explosion was close behind them. As he watched, the smoke and debris cleared behind them to reveal a clear road except for bits of debris that were the remains of their followers and their vehicles. It was then that an American fighter plane flew overhead and tipped its' wings in a victory salute. They had no idea what had exactly happened as the Military Police stopped just ahead of them and an armoured car circled and approached them from behind. They were trapped and the boys sat rigid expecting the worst as the

Military Police came to the pickup truck. They could not be sure that these police were not in the pay of their pursuers. "Goodchild and James I presume?" the M.P. in charge continued, "You will follow us to New York. There are some people there just dying to meet you." The boys were stunned. Who was waiting to meet them? Could it be the Russian agents? If it was they knew that their lifespan was now seriously limited. They had almost made it to relative safety only to be caught at the last moment. They turned their vehicle round and set off back up the road hemmed in by Police vehicles. They travelled along the tree lined back roads of New York State and all looked so tranquil and peaceful. Before they got to the city of New York the convoy turned onto another tree lined road and travelled for a few miles until they arrived at a security base. The road barriers were manned by armed guards which did nothing to ease the boys concerns. They were taken into a large administration building and shown into a spacious room furnished with tables and chairs and loungers. The room reminded Freddy of the N.A.A.F.I. back home. He could not help but feel that he would love to be back in that N.A.A.F.I. again now. The M.P. ordered them to sit, "You're going be here for some time guys, so make yourselves comfortable."

Armed guards stood at both ends of the room and all of the windows were barred so there was no chance of getting out. Neither of the boys felt immediately threatened so the idea of escape did not particularly appeal to them. The room was obviously used as a rest room and eating place for a large number of service people but from what the boys had observed as they arrived, a large number of people were no longer based at this unit. It must have been an air force or army base before its' present use. They lounged around and dozed from time to time during the twelve hours of waiting. During their wait they had been well fed and watered by service cooks. The food was very pleasant and there was plenty of it. They ate in silence and it was obvious to Freddy that Pinky was showing real signs of fatigue. He had never seen Pinky looking so tired and stressed. Pinky was renowned for his resilience in the face of any adversity. M.P.'s arrived to take Pinky out of the room leaving Freddy alone and feeling very apprehensive. His feeling did not last very long as minutes later the same thing happened to Freddy. He was taken along a series of corridors and shown into room which was furnished and had plush carpet from wall to wall. Sir George was in the room with some of his agents along with a lot of American top brass. Freddy had never seen such a display of scrambled egg and shiny medals. They sat at a very large polished table which reminded him of a court sitting in judgment. He had never been in a court room but he imagined that it must be like this. Was this the final act before they interrogated and then shot him? Freddy sat on a chair in the centre of the room facing them, not knowing how to cope with the situation and not knowing if they were friend or foe. The interrogators were not aggressive and they introduced themselves one by one and Freddy hoped against hope that these were the good guys and not his pursuers. They were all of respected official rank and they looked genuine but were they on the right side? He was asked his name, rank and number which he nervously gave them. Sir George started proceedings, "Relax Sgt. Goodchild your foreign pursuers have been dealt with. The officers here just need to know what happened to you following your last supply trip to Germany." Freddy was not fully convinced, "How do I know that I can trust you?" "You have no choice Goodchild, you must be aware that you do not exist and all records of you have been destroyed. We need to know if you were a willing party to this unfortunate and damaging series of events." Freddy thought for a while and realised the implications of what Sir George had just said and he was right, he had nothing to lose. He looked at the panel of interrogators in front of him and there was a look of sheer disbelief as he started to relate the recent events. It took a long time to relate the story of all that had happened to him and his friend but at the end of it the shock and surprise on the faces of his interrogators was a picture to see. His explanation was so comprehensive that there were no questions or challenges, everyone present was stunned by his story.

It was clear to all that the boys were totally innocent in the Cuban situation and had been forced to fly the aircraft with their cargo unwillingly. After reassurance by Sir George that they were not to be held at this base for long, Freddy was taken back to the room and Pinky joined him minutes later. When they were together again they realized that the wait had been some time because people had flown from England to find out how seriously the boys were involved. They were there nearly another hour during which time they discussed the sessions that they had just experienced and their thoughts on the outcomes. They were now both relieved to feel that they were in friendly hands and they felt more relaxed than they had been for some time. Sir George entered the room "Come on chaps, it's time for you to go home. You've had one hell of an experience and we don't want any delay in getting you both back home." They were taken by car to the city and driven directly onto the airfield where they took off from New York Idlewild Airport in a private Trans Atlantic jet. On the journey to the U.K. Sir George explained seriousness of the awkward situation that had emerged since their kidnapping and the discovery of the Cuban crisis. The implications of the events that involved them and their erasure from all personnel records and other records were very worrying. He explained that their understanding of it was the distinct possibly that there had been extensive infiltration of foreign agents into all Government agencies and therefore trust and reliability was undermined throughout the whole of the Government services. He told them that for safety reasons they were to stay with a trusted friend of Sir Georges' called Godfrey Bellinger who lived at Petersham Place in London. Godfrey was a long standing friend of Sir George and had come highly recommended as a trustworthy official. They were to stay at Petersham Place until further notice. He also informed them that members of their old aircrew had been very worried about them and instigated the search for them and it looked as if they owed their lives to them. It started to strike home to the boys just how close they were to death and it was only the timely intervention of the joint security services and American military that had saved their lives. The thought of their pursuers firing on them was fresh in their minds. 'Will the news of the U.S. Airforce taking out our pursuers be in the newspapers?" Asked Freddy. Sir George assured them that no one would be aware of the event, all news will be subject to a 'D' notice. They travelled nearly all the way in stunned silence, occasionally seeing the white tops of the waves in the Atlantic Ocean as they gazed out of the cabin windows. Knowing that they were now in safe hands and relatively safe did the shock really set in. The aircraft was no ordinary passenger plane, it had fully reclining seats, wide and very comfortable. It was fitted with a cafe and bar and carpeted cabin with lots of space to walk about. It appeared to be a very comfortable large lounge in the air. Tiredness overtook them both and they slept most of the way back to England. Freddy slipped into a sleep full of confusion and disturbing dreams. Foremost in his dreaming was the continuous pursuit and the outriders were disproportionate in size and threat, they dominated the many types of pursuers who were mostly shadows flitting throughout his ethereal pictures.

His memories pleasantly interupted the pursuit of the outriders when he recalled his uncle Derek buying his first motor bike. Derek came to his home in Park Lane to show off his 500cc BSA. He offered to take Freddy for a ride and asked him to get his wellies for the ride. It was autumn and the conker season, so Derek headed for a local river at Stokesley in Cleveland where the banks were lined with horse chestnut trees. A few conkers lay on the floor but many had been stood on or partially eaten by the wild life. The best lay in the shallow stream in the river, so Derek encouraged Freddy to go into the water to recover them. Freddy had his wellies on so all would be well, or so Freddy thought. As he stepped into the fiver the water was only half way up his wellies but as he tried to pick up the conkers the water rose and filled them with cold water. He travelled home with pockets full of conkers and his wellies containing soggy feet. In his disturbed dream the water rose above his wellies up to his waist, then chest, then above his head and Freddy woke in a panic. They were both relieved to see the coast of England and as they coasted in to land some of the tension lifted. The sight of the green fields and hamlets of the English countryside were pleasing to see and a wave of relief filled both Freddy and Pinky. They were driven quickly away from the airport heading for Godfrey Bellinger's house. Godfrey gave them a welcome and he seemed so relieved to see them, though he had never met either of them before. It was good to be back in England. They had a light supper and Godfrey was very interested in hearing their story while they ate. They soon were shown their rooms after telling Godfrey of their journey and they quickly retired for the night. They felt so refreshed after a good night's sleep. They had just finished breakfast when a car arrived to take them to see Sir George. As they travelled through the London city streets Freddy felt that they were being followed by a large black car. He thought that it must be his imagination and he put it down to his obsession with past events. Although he tried, Freddy could not shake off the feeling that they were still under surveillance by somebody. They arrived at Sir George's office and they were admitted by an aide straight away. "Good morning chaps we have had some of the paperwork from the Constellation translated and there is a wealth of information in there. Well done you two." Freddy interrupted "I may be being paranoid Sir George but I felt that we were being followed as we came here today." Sir George replied, "Quite correct young man, you are still being observed by our local Russian friends but how they got onto you so quickly I don't know. Let me tell you one of the main reasons that you were chosen. Pinky here was known to have been the test pilot on the delivery of the first Lockheed Constellation aircraft from the U.S.A. years ago and was therefore most likely competent in all eventualities for the delivery of the Russian missiles on that aircraft. They had to have someone experienced in flying that aircraft as they were stretching the plane to its' limits with the weight that they must have been carrying. It is down to him that you were kidnapped and all traces of your lives erased. Pinky was obviously totally oblivious to that of course and can't take any blame. Had the flight been caught you could tell your captors nothing and so you were not a risk to them. In the event that you succeeded you would be expendable and therefore they could make you disappear without trace. They very nearly succeeded but they did not expect you to survive their trap. I won't ask you how you escaped but it must have been something that only Pinky must have known about. The U.S. authorities could not explain it. They found the wreckage and some of the door remnants and they showed that the doors were very firmly sealed. By the way, the monies that you acquired are being held safely for your future use, it is the least that we can do for you. As you know, it confirms that there has been massive infiltration into all of our departments and armed services. We are in your debt for much of the knowledge that we now have but we still require your help. You are the only people who can recognise some of their agents involved. With your help we can access some of them and make inroads into discovering more of the agents who are working with them. To that end we want you to re-trace your steps from initial kidnap to the flight to Cuba. Will you do that for us?" The boys nodded and Sir George continued, "As you no longer exist you are no longer in the R.A.F. and therefore you will be on our staff until further notice. You will have London accommodation provided and all arrangements made for your general spending and living requirements. A car is waiting for you and one of our most trusted agents who will be working with you. You can leave by a secret exit from here and lose your friends out there. We will do our best to find out how they followed you so quickly. Good luck chaps, all of the other instructions are in the car." They were taken straight away to their new houses, avoiding any possibility of their being followed. They were extremely pleased with their Knightsbridge apartments and spent the morning rearranging things to their liking. They overlooked Hyde Park barracks and Hyde Park and the rear gardens were very private and not overlooked and the views from the front of the buildings were very pleasing and reassuring. The apartments were in a converted large house which was split into separate dwellings. Just after lunch the agent arrived from the ministry to introduce himself as Charles and he had instructions to take the boys through their recent travels, starting at Marham airbase. Charles presented them with an introductory letter from Sir George to confirm his identity. He was a fresh open faced young man of medium height but seen in public he would not have attracted any specific attention. He appeared very enthusiastic and keen to look after the boys on this mission. He appeared to be in his mid or late twenties and obviously fit and active. He was blond, not very tall and he was casually smartly dressed so that he would not have stood out in a crowd. He explained that he had been in the service now for a few years and had had a rapid move up in rank. Their objective was to learn as much as they could about any of the infiltrators. He described the plan of action by pointing out that the trail started from the boy's journeys to Germany. They would follow that and anywhere it may take them. As they left London Freddy observed the same black car following them again. "Charles, are you aware that we are being followed yet again?" "Yes they have been with us since we set off." Charles replied. Freddy asked, "Who knew that you were coming for us today?" "As far as I know, only Sir George but he must be working with a small ministry team. It might have got out from there but these agents seem to have had a source within our services for some time. I will let him know that there is a specific leak in one of the departments somewhere tipping off the Russians about your movements. Don't worry we will be losing them in a few minutes, I contacted the office via the car signaller and they should react very soon." They hadn't travelled very far when they saw a police car ahead driving very slowly with a stream of cars behind. People were very reluctant to overtake it and so it was towing a stream of cars. Charles accelerated and overtook the police car but as soon as the following black car overtook, the police car intercepted it bringing them to a halt. That was the last that they saw of the black car and its' occupants. Charles drove in to Upper Marham and then Burnthouse Drove Road. They soon stopped outside of the manor house near Lady's Wood. The manor gates were closed but they opened as Freddy applied gentle pressure.

Memories of their previous visit flooded back and they had a feeling of trepidation as the trio entered the large quadrangle but the place looked deserted and quite strange but how they were not sure. Things had not been disturbed but it looked strangely different and neglected. They quickly checked the areas familiar to them but there was nothing to be found. They stood in the kitchen at a loss and wondering what to do when they heard a muffled sound. No one was sure what it was or where it had originated but as Freddy opened the utility cupboard door they heard it again but louder. In the corner of the cupboard half hidden by the washing machine was Tom. He was trying to hide but the fear that he showed made him shake and groan. "Hello Tom it is only us, there is nothing to be afraid of. Where is Alan?" asked Freddy. Tom hesitated but recognition showed on his face as the fear subsided. "I don't know I only work here. I've always worked here. I thought that they had come back. They threw me out and told me to go away but I sneaked back in and hid here. This is my home. I have nowhere else to go. I heard that Ali man arguing with Alan. There was lots of shouting and then I heard shots being fired. I don't know where Alan is and I haven't seen him since they left. I have nowhere else to go, I have always lived here with Alan I don't know anything other." Tom sounded very shocked and confused. They left Tom for a while in the kitchen having checked that all the food was still there but they soon came back having found no trace of Alan. "So where is everyone Tom?" Pinky asked. "They were all here this morning and then I heard all the shouting. Just after that they all left and I thought it might have been them coming back when I heard you arriving. As they left I heard Ali say something about Whitehall but I don't know of any White Hall near here." "They must be heading for London and if they are going to Whitehall that means that they must have a contact or contacts in the Ministry. Where was the shouting coming from Tom?" Freddy asked. Tom replied "From Alan's office down the corridor there." Tom pointed to the far door in the kitchen. "Come on chaps, we haven't looked down here." Freddy set off through the door and into a long corridor with small rooms to the left and right. When they ate in the kitchen before, Freddy thought that the door leading to this corridor was just a cupboard door and did not realise that there was anything of interest here. Only one room at the end contained anything other than rubbish. This was obviously Alan's office and there was blood all over the floor. The place was full of files and papers but the desk and surrounding area was clear. Charles left them to look for any other signs of violence anywhere in the building. Charles set off through the out buildings looking into all the rooms that had been occupied by staff members at some time. He went into the main building and marvelled at the faded splendour but he found nothing significant. Back outside he headed for the boiler room and as he passed the coal cellar he spotted the sprawling form of a blood covered body. "That must be Alan." thought Charles. He checked the pockets of the sad figure and found a driving license with a photograph, confirming his fears. Meanwhile Freddy and Pinky searched through the papers in and on Alan's desk. Freddy came across Alan's 'bait tin'. Freddy thought that he had kept his sandwiches in it. That had always puzzled Freddy as the kitchen was always well stocked and Alan didn't seem to go anywhere very often. Why did he need a 'Bait tin'? Freddy was curious and opened the tin to find that if was full of papers and documents. One of the documents was Alan's last will and testament. Freddy glanced through it and found that Alan had left the manor house and a considerable amount of money to Tom. He was the only beneficiary. Freddy had good news for Tom. Charles arrived into

Alan's office and told them that he had found the body of a male in his fifties shot through the head and dumped into the coal cellar. It had to be Alan. The trio went back to the kitchen where they found Tom still in a daze. Freddy gently roused Tom and gave him the good news, "You won't need to go anywhere now Tom this is all yours. This is your home." Tom was clutching a photograph and Freddy asked Tom what it was. The question seemed to bring Tom back to reality, "This is Alan and the baby is me. He was like a father to me. When I grew up I did odd jobs for Alan and got pocket money for looking after the rooms upstairs and any visitors that came. We had lots and lots of people coming here but not as many now. I got a lot of pocket money to look after you." "Look," said Freddy "those awful men won't be coming back and they won't hurt you again. If they had wanted to harm you they would have done that before they left. We will be sending some men here to look through all of Alan's papers but they are good guys, so don't worry. Is there anyone that we could contact to stay with you for a while?" Tom shook his head. Freddy continued, "We will be leaving very soon but you will be fine and we will come back to see you before too long." They said goodbye to Tom and set off back to London. It seemed that for a change they were not being followed and they returned to London without incident. Although they had assured Tom that he would be alright, none of them was totally convinced about that. Sir George was waiting for them in his office, "I understand that you have found more information for me." Charles reported, "Firstly Sir, we were followed from this office all the way to Marham." "That is impossible," exploded Sir George, "that must mean that there is a leak from this department. Only a handful of people knew of your mission and none of my aids were told. It must have been somebody in the security management team or someone very close to them.. I can't believe that someone on my committee has been compromised." "It is the only explanation, however, I did send you that information by radio earlier today" Charles added. "I agree," said Freddy "we have been followed ever since we got back to 'Blighty'. They knew where we were staying and we were even observed at Petersham Place. Someone very close to you has been supplying the Russian agents with all details of our movements." Charles interrupted "There is a lot of paperwork at the manor house and from what little I read, there is some very valuable information in them. I suggest that I take some of the boys in my team to go through it all immediately, not forgetting what the boys told me about Jones in the Customs office. Let the boys lie low for a while Sir." "Good idea," said Sir George "I will be back in touch with you boys when Charles gets all the information back to me and we will take it from there. Your message was not passed on to me so I will check on that. Use only the red priority communications Charles and nobody but you and I will know the content of what you find." The trio left the office and Charles dropped the boys and the car off at Kings Cross Station and they all took the underground moving from train to train at the last minute to avoid any chance of anyone being able to follow them. They finally left the underground at Battersea station and the boys followed Charles who moved at pace. They went into a car salesroom building and Charles acknowledged the man in the sales office. They left the building by a rear door. Out from the back door they turned right into an alleyway and at the far end they came to a lockup garage which Charles opened and they went in to find a windowless van. Charles drove the van out of the garage with the boys out of sight in the back. They travelled for about fifteen minutes and came to a stop. The van doors opened and the boys found themselves inside of a very large warehouse. They followed Charles up some stairs to an upper floor where Charles opened a door to reveal a spacious, fully furnished apartment. The door leading into the flat was a heavily barred metal door with a spy hole at head height. "This is your temporary home and you will find everything you need in here, follow me. I spent some time here and though it is a back water warehouse there are plenty of things to do" The boys followed Charles into one of many side rooms as Charles explained that this was a high security safe house. "In this room there is every sort of disguise that you can imagine in a kit and as you are free to come and go as you please make sure that you are not recognized. Try out the disguises they are very good. If you need to contact me just use the radio here. It is a single frequency unit outside of all public wave bands and untraceable." Charles left the boys, promising that he or a trusted agent would check on them at eight- o-clock every morning. He asked them to be sure that no one was allowed to know that they were staying here. He would do his best to keep their whereabouts safe. After a good night's sleep the boys explored the apartment and the many side rooms. They played around and had great fun with many of the disguises. The day seemed to pass very quickly and they were not concerned that Charles had not visited them this morning. After all he had only left them late last night. They settled down to a relaxing drink in the evening to watch the television but there was the usual rubbish on TV so they chatted and reviewed the recent happenings. The drink flowed and they became rather morose as bed time approached. Charles arrived promptly at eight-o-clock the next morning to make sure that all was well. Charles was correct when he said that there was everything they needed in their 'Suite' as the boys called it. There were clothes, food, drink, money and lots of entertainment. There were six large bedrooms each with shower and toilet. Charles stayed for a while and told them what had been found at the manor but after he had left them they had a great time trying out some more of the disguises, whiskers, hair pieces and amongst the many clothing outfits, tramps clothing and lots of pieces of string. As they experimented in front of the bathroom mirror with different characters, laughing at the incredible changes, Pinky noticed a lever next to the toilet and traced the attached wire to a catch above the large bathroom window. "Hey have you seen this," said Pinky "this is where they must have brought in all the large pieces of furniture. If we pull this lever the whole window will come out." They opened a small window within the large window to reveal a pulley operated platform that could be controlled by the person on the platform. "Cool." Freddy quipped. They had lunch and then listened to the radio. The news was dominated by the Cuban crisis, relations between the Americans and the Russians had deteriorated. The boys felt some guilt and responsibility for the situation but tried some distraction, playing a game of cards. The evening seemed to drag on and on until they went to their beds. Charles called the next morning right on time with news of some progress from Sir George. The paperwork from the manor house had given clues to many of the junior infiltrators who were now all under investigation by security services. Charles left them after a while and as he closed and locked the door Freddy said, "Let's try out some of these disguises and get out of here for a while. What about this evening going to a local pub and having drink and a pub meal?"

"Yes," replied Pinky "I'd love a change of scenery with a large ice cold gin and tonic. That is one thing lacking in this place, ice." They played around with more disguises and had a good laugh at some of the characters that they created. One that stood out as a 'must try' were a couple of post men's outfits. They put on wigs, whiskers and eyebrow extensions and when they looked in the bathroom mirror at their reflections they both agreed that they both looked the part. They left in disguise mid evening as it was getting dark. They walked to the end of the road and there were pubs left and right.  The one on the left seemed quieter so they headed for that one, In the King's Head they spent a very pleasant evening playing darts and dominoes with the locals who seemed to accept them for who they were supposed to be without question, two postmen. They got back to the warehouse suite without incident and they were quite excited that they had fitted in to the pub crowd as two postmen. They could not wait to tell Charles all about it in the morning. The boys were up and dressed by seven-o-clock the next morning and they had just cleared away breakfast when the doorbell rang. It wasn't the usual signal so Freddy checked who it was at the door through the spy hole. Charles was standing there with the strangest look of surprise on his face. Freddy unlocked and opened the door but as he did, Charles fell forward into Freddy's arms and as Freddy caught him the thugs burst past him into the suite. Charles was dead and Freddy lowered his body to the floor. Charles still had thaat innocent surprised look on his face, like a child full of wonderment, questioning what he saw. They had been taken completely by surprise by the seven intruders and Ali was amongst them. Freddy recognised him immediately and noticed that he was the only one of them who was not carrying a firearm. Two armed men grabbed hold of Freddy and another two held Pinky. Ali broke the stunned silence, "You have caused us a lot of trouble and cost us a number of our agents. You will tell us what you took from the manor house and what you already know, you will tell us everything." From the way Ali was talking he didn't know anything about the papers on the aircraft. Freddy blurted out, "We only know what you told us, we know nothing more." Ali slapped Freddy across his face, "Liar! You took papers from the house, the boy told us." Pinky interjected, "The man who took the papers is the one that you have just murdered." Ali walked slowly over to Pinky and taking a gun out of his associates jacket he hit Pinky on the chin with the butt of the handgun causing a gash to open up on the point of his Pinky's chin and he slumped forward unconscious. Blood flowed out of Pinky's chin as he laid on the floor. Pinky groaned as he quickly started to regain his senses. "Look Ali, I'll tell you all I know and this sort of thing is not necessary. Let me take Pinky to the bathroom to clean him up and we will tell you all we know about the things that we have discovered." Ali agreed to let Freddy take Pinky to the bathroom but they were escorted by two of the thugs. The other intruders were sent to look round the suite for any information the boys may have hidden. Ali slumped onto a settee, "Don't be long boys I don't like to be kept waiting." Freddy nearly carried Pinky along the corridor to the bathroom where he sat him on the toilet seat whilst he went to the sink for a face cloth and towel. The two gunmen went to the window to look for any chance of possible escape out of the window. Suddenly there was a great loud crash as the heavy window frame fell from its' mounting crashing down on top of the gunmen. One of the men was dead on impact as the window handle crashed through his chest cavity killing him instantly. The other gunman was rendered completely unconscious. Pinky had timed the pull of the lever next to the toilet to perfection, catching both men totally unaware and leaving them no chance of avoiding the full weight of the metal and glass window. The noise of the crash was partially cushioned by the gunmen and the rest of the gunmen were too far away to hear anything to arouse alarm. Freddy handed the wet cloth to Pinky to wipe the worst of the blood away. On inspection the cut was not as bad as first thought but the flow of blood made it look like a serious injury. Some of the disguises were still in the bag in the bathroom when they had  been messing about the previous day. "You grab the make-up tin Pinky and I'll bring the rest of the stuff." Without delay they left the bathroom by the window climbing onto the pulley platform outside. Freddy turned the pulley handle as fast as he could and they reached the ground in seconds. They were at the rear of the warehouse in the loading yard. Freddy remembered the shed that was on a piece of spare ground next to the Kings Head, "Quick this way we'll head for that shed near the Kings Head. Are you alright Pinky?" "I'll make it." He replied. They made it to the shed without any problems. The door was wide open as they reached it and they shut it as soon as they were inside. The smell was awful but in the circumstances it was of little consequence. The bleeding had stopped after keeping the pressure of the towel for some time applied to Pinky's chin. His face was a bit of a mess, "You need some whiskers to cover that lot up so let's make up as the tramps and it will not be obvious to anyone looking closely at you that you have had any injury. It is also fitting as tramps in this place, it stinks." They worked on their disguises and with each other's help and lots of string, they really looked the part. When they were fully disguised Pinky sat on an upturned beer crate and Freddy on a pile of sacks in the corner. They planned to wait until dark before they ventured out to allow the Russian group to complete their search. No doubt the Russians were checking everywhere for them by now. The noise of people running and shouting got closer and closer and the boys held their breaths. The door smashed open and a gun waving Ali was framed in the doorway. The speed of the opening door caused an uncontrolled look of surprise on the occupants faces and Ali saw, what apppeared to be, two down and out tramps of little consequence. In his fury Ali thought to rid the world of such low life but he realised that the sound of his gun would attract too much attention and his quarry would be lost for good. The boys feared the worst but Ali was hit by the smell and saw two old tramps squatting in a shed, he cursed and left without delay. The unbelieving pair stared at each other in stunned silence. They couldn't believe their good fortune, they had completely fooled Ali and his gang and as the noise faded they got to their feet and carefully left the shed. They took their disguise kit with them knowing they might really need it again. It took a lot of nerve to slowly shamble down the street away from the warehouse. Every sinew in their body wanted to flee as fast as they could but they maintained their shambling gait all the way to the underground station. They were heading for Sir George and a promise of some security. They were not completely sure that Sir George wasn't the leak but they had to take the chance that he was not the traitor as he was their only contact. At the ministry they had difficulty persuading the guard who they were but as they removed some of the whiskers he let them pass and they were taken to Sir George's office. "No one knew where we were, how did the Russian group know? It has to be someone very close to you or the only other explanation is that you are the leak Sir George," accused Freddy and he continued without waiting for a reply "Charles was murdered on the information given by whoever is The infiltrator." He continued and told Sir George the whole story of events at the warehouse. Sir George did not react other than to repeat over and over, "My God!" From Sir George's reactions it was plain to see that he was totally devastated by the story of what had happened to them and in particular the death of Charles. His head swam with the thoughts that began to become clear to him and the implications were unthinkable. Eventually he gathered himself to speak "You boys have been very resourceful and I am so pleased that you are okay after what you have been through. You are absolutely correct to suspect me as we don't know who we can trust. Charles was my nephew and I just don't know how I'm going to break the news to my brother. Would you two like to get out of that gear? You can use my private bathroom through there. Please use any clothing that you find suitable in my wordrobe. The boys  returned later smelling a lot sweeter and looking more like themselves but events  had left marks on them both. Sir George was pouring a large whisky as the boys came back, "I am sure that you could do with a snifter as much as me." He poured two more large whiskies and continued "you took the right action and I am proud that you had the gumption to doubt me as well but you can be assured that we are reading from the same song sheet. You are right that it must be someone very close to me who is the traitor. We took every precaution to make sure that no one outside of our meetings could possibly overhear or record our planning. You chaps must have someone in mind seeing as you took the risk of coming back here?" He drained his glass and looked unblinking at the boys. Freddy answered "We went through all of the committee members but there was no one who could possibly know of all of our movements the one common factor is Petersham Place. No one knew that we were there at the beginning but we were followed as soon as we left the house. How did they know when no one on our side knew? When Charles picked us up to go to Marham we were followed from the off. Who knew? To check on any of our suspicions we need to set a trap. Whoever it responsible is masterminding their operations from this district." They decided to leave the final planning until the morning and Sir George offered them overnight accommodation in his office suite guest rooms. As they prepared to retire for the night the telephone rang and a voice at the other end told Sir George that Godfrey Bellinger was here to see him. Sir George agreed to see him and after a few minutes there was a knock at the door. "Come in Godfrey." said Sir George and as Godfrey came into the room he was startled to see the boys sitting there. "What is it Godfrey?" asked Sir George. It took Godfrey a few seconds to recover from his shock, "I came to tell you that young Cubby is trying to contact Freddy and Pinky about a re-union and I was going to ask you to pass on the message when you saw them again. I thought it better to deliver the message in person rather than risk a phone call." Sir George was thoughtful and  finally said "Tell Cubby to call at my office first thing in the morning and I will make arrangements for them to meet up. Thank you Godfrey." It was the signal for Godfrey to leave so he bade them goodnight and left the office. The interruption awakened them all and they decided to have another night cap. As they sipped their whiskies Sir George said "I have been thinking and I have my doubts about Sir Aubrey Witheringshaw. If I let him and only him know about tomorrow's meeting with Cubby then if things go wrong we have our culprit." "Well you may be right Sir but we also know that Godfrey knows, why not just leave it at that and at least clear Godfrey. Involving someone else now may cloud the issue." "You are right Freddy as things stand it will be clear cut. Well chaps let's call it a night." They set off for a much needed night's sleep. The guest rooms were superior to any hotel that the boys had experienced and the fridge was fully stocked and lacked any price tags. The next morning Cubby arrived at the ministry quite early and was shown in to see Sir George. The boys were in the next office waiting for the signal to go in to meet Cubby. "Good morning Cubby, do sit down. Now tell me about this re-union that you want to arrange." Sir George sat down behind his desk. Cubby told the story of the crew and their regular meetings and how they planned if and when they were separated to keep up the tradition of getting back together on a regular basis. Godfrey had told Cubby that the boys were back and in London and the crew had come to London to meet up with them and get the story of recent events. "Well," said Sir George and the boys came in at the signal "you had better talk to them yourself." The boys greeted Cubby and said that they would like to get back with the crew and as agreed with Sir George they would meet that afternoon at the 2i's Coffee Bar in Wardour Street. Cubby was delighted to see the boys in good spirits and questioned if it was a good idea for them to meet after hearing a little about recent events. He was assured that it fitted their plans exactly. They chatted for a short time and Sir George broke up the meeting so that he could talk to the boys. Cubby left and Sir George then said "We will be in force looking out for you this afternoon in the event that an attempt is made on you at the Coffee Bar. The waiting about was the worst but at the appointed time the boys arrived in Wardour Street and went downstairs in the 2i's. The crew was already there and a rowdy cheer went up at the sight of the boys coming down to the cellar. "At least we are too early for the music," said Pinky "so we can have a good old chat." The meeting went on for a good two hours and they were all full of coffee by the time they parted with promise of another get together soon. The crew had been partially included in the past events but they had only a very limited knowledge of the implications. The boys left Wardour Street and headed for Picadilly Circus and then on to the ministry. They had not seen any of the backup promised by Sir George but no doubt it was there somewhere. Back in Sir George's office Sir George said "I am pleased to report that there were no incidents or sightings anywhere during your meeting so that rules out Godfrey." The phone rang and it was Godfrey "I have Cubby here for you Sir George." "Hello Sir. Godfrey was saying that he thought it might be alright for Freddy and Pinky to come to Petersham Place this evening. The crew and I have decided to have a quiet drink together and they may be staying over for the night?" "Well I can't see any problem with that, just hold," and he asked the boys if they were agreed "yes that seems to be in order they will be on their way shortly." Sir George put the phone down. "I will send an escort with you at a discreet distance just in case and we will keep a watch if you chose to stay overnight. Have fun boys." They left and headed to Petersham Place in a ministry car followed at a distance by the escort car. They arrived at Godfrey's to be greeted by Cubby and Godfrey on the doorstep. There was much back slapping and cheery greetings when they met the crew again and the questions came fast and furious from the crew members. The boys could not answer some of the queries as they were security sensitive. Godfrey had gone to another part of the building to allow the chaps to chat and reminisce and it was all alien talk to him anyway he had said. The boys had a final drink before leaving and they were preparing to go when the front door smashed open sending splintering wood flying all around. Ali and a group of armed men burst into the house and a volley of gun fire was heard throughout the house. Freddy and Pinky hit the ground at the same time and each wondered if the other had been shot. Shots continued to ring out and the boys lay on the ground for what seems like an age until silence took over, Freddy raised his head and gave an audible gasp. The room and entrance passage were quiet and Freddy could the dead forms of Ali and his gang on the floor. Sir George stood in the doorway and shouted "Is everybody ok?" The crew gradually got to their feet stunned by what had just happened and the reply came from weak voices "We think so." Sir George asked "Is that the famous Ali?" Ali was laid on the floor in a most unnatural position, "Yes that's him," replied Freddy. "Right let's get you all out of here," said Sir George and turned to leave but suddenly stopped "Where is Godfrey?" No one had seen him during all the noise and confusion so a search was made by the security men and he was discovered unconscious on the upstairs landing. Sir George roused him and made sure that he was alright before he left for the ministry with the boys. At the ministry Sir Aubrey was being held in the interrogation room. He had been informed about the 2i's meeting and even though nothing had happened there he was being questioned anyway. The security team had worked on him all night but Sir Aubrey maintained that he had not divulged the information to anyone. Eventually he was released under house arrest. The boys remained at the ministry building but they did not see any of the security service team including Sir George. The boys felt as if they were under house arrest as they were not allowed out of the building for their own safety. Later that evening there was a knock on their door. The door opened and Sir George entered "Well chaps, we have been all day checking on Sir Aubrey's movements and contacts and we have drawn a total blank. It seems to be as he told us because it seems impossible for him to have been in touch with anyone. All his calls and activities have been monitored from the time I told him to the time we arrested him. I think that you and I will have to go and have another chat to him." The boys set off with Sir George, pleased at last to get out of the ministry building. They were driven under escort to Sir Aubrey's house in Knightsbridge. As they approached his house there was something very wrong. There were security cars in numbers outside of his house and the door was wide open. Sir George leapt from the car as it came to a halt with the boys in pursuit. They went in through the open door and were taken upstairs by one of the security agents to Sir Aubrey's bed room. There on the bed lay Sir Aubrey who was clearly dead with half of his head blown away by gunshot. He was still grasping a heavy gage weapon in his right hand still pointing to the side of his head that had been blown away. "Well chaps, I don't know how he did it but it looks like a clear cut expression of guilt. He must have known that we were on to him and he committed suicide." Sir George concluded. He turned to leave and then stopped in his tracks "That's all wrong," he said "he was left handed and a bullet of that caliber would be small entry and large exit site. His right index finger is on the trigger and he suffered from Dupuytrens syndrome in his right hand the index finger on the trigger was totally rigid and could not possibly have fired the gun. This is a murder case. Search the room for any clues that could tell us who else was here. Come on chaps let's leave them to get on with it." They left the building and set off back to the ministry with their escort. Back in the office Sir George reviewed the situation "This puts a totally different complexion on this. Sir Aubrey was completely innocent but someone wanted us to think otherwise. How did this get out when no one else knew about it?" They sat a while thinking things through when Freddy suddenly said "I have been thinking about all of the incidents involving pursuers since we arrived back in England and I hope that you chaps can prove me wrong. The only person who has been the common factor in all of this is Cubby's cousin Godfrey Bellinger. I know that we found him unconscious at his house but was he genuine or was it purely for us to see? Was he just putting it on? We didn't see any injury on him." Sir George and Pinky stared at him. After some thought Sir George said "You may have a point Freddy but I hope that you are wrong, even so we cannot discount or disprove what you say so we will have to change our thinking and adopt a different emphasis." Sir George picked up the phone to call Godfrey "Hello Godfrey, how are you? Great so can you come around to my office in the morning to discuss some new information that we have discovered. First thing will be fine." The following morning they boys were in Sir George's office early waiting for Godfrey to arrive when an agent involved in yesterday evening's events knocked on the office door. Sorry to bother you sir but we got a call from Godfrey Bellinger a few minutes ago asking about Sir Aubrey Witheringshaw and the chap who answered told him that he had been murdered. We called at his house to bring him here as arranged but the house was deserted and much of Bellinger's personal belongings were missing." "Thank you agent Blaze you can stand down," Sir George waved his hand dismissing the agent and continued "It looks as if you were correct Freddy we have our leak." He picked up the phone and asked records to do a full check on the background of Godfrey Bellinger without delay. Fifteen minutes later a secretary handed a file to Sir George. He sat reading it intently for a while and suddenly he thumped the desk "I'll have someone's head for this, incompetence, absolute bloody incompetence. Godfrey worked with John Cairncross in the ministry of supply in fifty seven. Cairncross worked with Kim Philby and they are both suspected double agents and under ongoing investigation. This should have been picked up years ago. We have to find Godfrey without delay it looks like we have found the hub of the infiltration of Russian agents. We are investigating the content of messages sent by Cairncross and Philby and while nothing seems amiss with the content security have uncovered possible code within the coding used. All the messages were sent through Berlin where your friend Ali was based. This is just one big mess and we would not have the leads that we have now if it had not been for you boys. You have opened a 'Pandoras box' giving us a massive job ahead to identify these traitors. That fool of an agent who informed Bellinger of our knowledge of the murder alerted him to the fact that we weren't fooled by their set up. He knew straight away that we would suspect him now that Sir Aubrey was known to be an innocent victim. You chaps have been invaluable in this matter and I hope that you are going to see this thing through? In fact I hope that you will be happy to come onto our staff being fully employed in security." Freddy and Pinky looked at each other and nodded their agreement. "Thank Sir." They both said. "Well done chaps welcome aboard. Now you two must lay low and out of circulation for a while until we make sure that you are no longer prime targets. The next day the boys sat in the ministry building apartment "We can't just sit around here all the time," said Freddy "let's get out before I lose my sanity. We can get out disguise kit out and see what we can do." They both agreed and played around with different disguise characters applying false noses, moustaches and eyebrows. With clear glass spectacles they effected a complete transformation. They spend the rest of the day walking around and exploring London town. They were acutely aware that they may be being followed so they took a variety of evasive actions but they saw nothing suspicious and were sure that they were alone. They got back to the ministry late evening and entered using the passes arranged before they left. The guard was very suspicious as he did not recognise them but the passes were effective. They had just removed their disguises when Sir George entered. "Hello chaps. Godfrey has flown the coop. He left early this morning as we were learning that he was no longer at his home. He left by plane from London City Airport and we have a team there looking for any information that might lead us to his whereabouts. His flight was tracked to Berlin but he appears to have parachuted just before they made Berlin airspace. We must go and find him." "We were roped into this at the beginning by Carl," said Freddy "he worked in the mess at our Berlin supply base he must have had contact with their operation in Germany. He may not know about events here in the U.K. so he may not know what our involvement is now. If we talk to him then we might get some good leads as to where Godfrey might be." "Good plan," said Sir George "we'll set off first thing tomorrow. I will arrange the flight tonight and we will get to Germany before lunch time. Leave it all to me. My aide will give you a morning call." Sir George left them and they looked at each other with the joint feeling of 'here we go again.' Early the next morning they set off in a private jet to Germany. They had driven straight onto the air strip and boarded straight from the car. They were both thankful that there wasn't a long car journey to the airport this time. They landed at the air force base and went straight to the mess. They asked for Carl but they were told that he hadn't been seen for a week failing to do his shifts and being threatened with dismissal when he did show up. They asked where they could find him and reluctantly the mess manager gave them the last known address for Carl. Sir George made a quick telephone call from the mess and as they left a car pulled up at the door followed by two escort vehicles. They got into the leading car and headed for Carl's last known address which was a farm only ten minutes from the air base. The driver was local and knew the farm well. The farm looked as if it had not been tended for years and the outbuildings were in a very run down state. As they drew up to the farmhouse they could see that the farm door was wide open and as they went in it was clear that the farm had not been occupied for days. "Check all the rooms and outhouses for anything that could help us locate Carl." Sir George ordered. Freddy checked the fire place to see if there was any warmth in the hearth. As he knelt down to feel the coals in the grate he could see the soot covered back plate on the chimney. The fire was cold but as he looked closer Freddy could see written in the soot 'Zeestow Kirche'. "Have a look at this Sir George it means nothing to me but maybe it is what we are looking for." Sir George bent down to look 'Zeestow Kirche'." he said. "What was that Sir?" said one of the escorts and Sir George repeated "'Zeestow Kirche'." "I know it well Sir," said the agent "it is not far from Berlin near Wustermark." "Ok, let's go." said Sir George and he made for the door. The convoy headed for Berlin and had only been travelling for a few minutes when four motor cycles caught up with them and drew alongside the boy's car. The bikers opened fire with handguns but as the car was bullet proof they came to no harm as the doors and windows were sprayed with bullets. The two escort cars immediately returned fire and three of the bikers died before they hit and bounced along the road. The fourth and last biker wobbled along the road for some was before going off the road and crashing into the trees lining the road. The rear escort car stopped and two agents went to see where the biker was. They found him barely conscious but obviously dying. They asked him in German who had sent him and he barked a venomous response which proved to be too much effort and his spirit departed from his mortal remains. "Did he say anything?" Sir George asked.

"Nothing sir just a nasty curse in Russian." Sir George made a quick phone call and they all got back to their vehicles and continued on their way. Freddy enquired about the phone call and Sir George informed them that he had contacted the 'Tidy Team'. "They will make sure that the dead attackers will be taken before anyone spots them and makes a nuisance of themselves." They arrived at the church in Zeestow as the light was fading. The armed escort entered the church first but the building was empty. The church and the back rooms offered no clues as to the whereabouts of Carl. "Where do we go from here?" Freddy asked Sir George. He ordered another search of the interior and exterior of the building but no matter how hard they tried they couldn't find a thing. The place was clean, possibly too clean. Someone had used the building but then had it very professionally cleaned. No finger prints on anything, no litter, nothing. They decided to leave and move on to Berlin in the hope of finding some clues there. Freddy was last to leave but as he was closing the door he heard 'tip,tip,tip' 'tap,tap,tap' 'tip,tip,tip' it was the sound of metal on metal. He called to Sir George and when he arrived back he told him to listen. Freddy said "It is Morse code Sir S.O.S." "By God you're right" he replied "Get everyone back I want that noise traced now." Freddy went to the nearest radiator and tapped loudly. The response was immediate. "There's someone wherever the boiler is located Sir." The order was given to find a cellar or boiler room quickly. It took a while for one of the agents to find a stone trap door in the vestry. The trap door was a heavy concrete slab and took two people to lift it. Stone steps led down below the church itself. Agents with torches ventured down the stone steps to a dark cellar below and found Carl, his wife and two children chained to the heating pipes. Carl had been tapping his chains on the pipe in the hope that someone would hear his S.O.S. He had been tapping constantly for days not knowing if it was day or night down in the depths of the church. He was very weak and his family was in a very distressed condition and were in need of urgent medical help. Freddy found a light switch and luckily there was still an electricity supply. The cellar burst into bright light. Carl recognised Pinky and Freddy immediately "I thought that they had killed you both. Thank God they didn't and you came after me. My family and I owe you our lives." Freddy asked him "Who brought you here?" "They brought us here just after you picked up your last load of cigarettes and whisky. You had just left when a gang of Russian speaking gunmen forced me into a car. They took me to the farm and picked up Helga and the children. I overheard them mention Zeestow and the church and left a message for anyone to find. They brought us straight here and we've been here until you arrived a few minutes ago. Some hours ago now they came back and one of the Russians came back to kill us but an English man told him to put his gun away. He did not want anyone to know that they were here and the noise might attract attention." Freddy continued "Did you know the English man?" "No but I heard them talking about getting to East Berlin and one of the Russians called him Billinner." "Could it have been Bellinger?" asked Freddy. Carl smiled and nodded. The escort agents got them released from their chains and made arrangements for them to be taken to hospital for a checkup and then home. Carl's involvement was not a matter for British Security. They left Carl and his family with lots of hugs and kisses from the girls and as they travelled on to Berlin Sir George updated them. "You two still have no identities you still don't exist so we have to do something about that without delay. I propose to give you new identities with bank accounts and everything you need to provide a history for yourselves. Our northern agent has stood down in retirement now after his last mission to find you both. His imaginary identity is now vacant but the name carries history and essentials. You can become the brothers Huntley G. Haverstock and Huntley J. Haverstock." Pinky interrupted "Thank you sir but after this is all over I propose to retire as well. I was thinking of retiring from the R.A.F. before all of this and after all that has happened I am more than sure now." "Well if you are sure Pinky, "said Sir George "you know that the rewards are very good and with benefits but if I can't change your mind?" "No," replied Pinky "I think that I could do with putting my feet up from now on." "In that case we will make sure that your future needs in retirement are taken care of." As Sir

George continued talking to Freddy, Pinky cast his mind back to the time in married quarters and his life with Mary. Soon after the war finished Pinky met his childhood sweetheart and they soon wed. They got accommodation in married quarters and they tried for a family but their efforts were not productive. His brother had three children and the Air force life meant that contact with family was very unusual. His wife Mary died after a severe stroke and his loss made him yearn for family. This was his chance to contact what family he had left and he was determined to take this chance to retire. He was soon to be retired from the R.A.F. anyway and this was the sooner prospect. Freddy was quite happy to continue the tradition as Huntley G. Haverstock and though Sir George was prepared to drop the G. which was no longer required for identification, Freddy was quite happy with it. Sir George said that all would be in place before they got back to England. As they entered West Berlin their car was stopped by a sergeant M.P. "Sir George?" he enquired. Sir George nodded. "We have a message for you from a double agent in East Berlin. It makes no sense to us but I am sure that it is important sir. Agent Stiller wants to defect to the West and he has sent this note to aid his cause." He handed the note to Sir George and he read it very carefully, "Thank you sergeant that is all. This is an old code but it appears that Godfrey has been in touch with the Eastern Block agency and is looking for their help to cross over immediately from West Berlin to East Berlin. He has given his position at a known safe house in Friedrich Strasse near the station. Driver, if you know this place, then let's go. We don't want him getting across the wall." The driver knew the place well as it was near a regular exchange point at the bridge in Friedrich Strasse. As they headed there they were joined by two more escort cars filled with armed agents. Friedrich Strasse was still showing the damage from the allied bombing of World War II. They arrived at a bomb site rubble strewn area close to the safe house and the place was surrounded before Sir George and the occupants of the new cars went in unannounced. They were not challenged or impeded by the Russian agents who were inside. They all had legitimate reasons for being there, sanctioned by the West Berlin authorities. There was no sign of Bellinger. The Russian agents gave them no sensible answers to their questions and they gave no indication that they knew what Sir George was talking about. Sir George respected the training that these agents had undergone and he knew that any further interogation at this time would not help their immediate need to find the whereabouts of Godfrey. Suddenly Freddy saw Bellinger out of the rear window running across the open ground at the back of the house. Two of Sir George's men appeared and Bellinger opened fire on the one nearer to him hitting the agent in the thigh. As the agent fell to the ground Bellinger ran into a hail of bullets, killing him instantly. Sir George was furious, he wanted Bellinger alive "Take this lot and incarcerate them." The Russian agents were led away and they made no fuss as they knew that they would not be held for long. Sir George turned and left the building knowing that they could do no more in Berlin. Before they reached the car the Sergeant M.P. handed another note to Sir George from Stiller. He thanked his German escort team for all of their help and the trio was taken to the nearest airfield where they took off for home. They were all disappointed that Bellinger had died in the exchange as he had information that would have expedited their search for the other agents. Not much was said but Sir George appeared to sit the whole journey fuming and muttering to himself. The boys had never seen him behave in such a way and they were very concerned to see him like this. When they got back Freddy and Pinky moved into two pleasant and spacious furnished apartments above an Italian restaurant on Victoria Embankment yards away from the Houses of Parliament. Whitehall was just around the corner. There was talk that the Government had future plans to take the whole block over but nothing had ever happened. It was a pleasant change to be away from the ministry and the feeling of freedom was a tonic. The next few days turned into weeks of pleasant freedom and fun. Soho and all the mysteries of the area became second nature to them. They had a more relaxing time in the 2i's than they had the first time that they had been there. They regularly visited it and listened to the well known singers and performers that appeared nightly in the music bar such as Vince Eager and the Vagabonds, Wee Willie Harris, Ricky Towns and a new duo from Newcastle called Nivram, later to become known as the Shadows. They enjoyed the shows that appeared in the many of the theatres in the district. Life was good. They had plenty of money and they enjoyed each other's company. The memories of Germany etc. were beginning to fade and after a relaxing evening in town they were preparing to retire for the night when there was a knock on Freddy's door. Freddy opened the door to see Sir George standing there "Come in Sir." Freddy said. "Sorry to call at such a late hour but I needed you to be put in the picture. You will remember as we left Berlin we received a communication from Stiller in East Berlin. It contained a message within the message. I have the results of the de-coding. It seems that Bellinger was the deputy director of operations in England and in charge of a large number of Russian agents many of whom we have now arrested. It means that the director is still operating. That means that you two are still at risk. They still need to know what information you have and what you took in the paperwork that you found. The people who could tell them are now dead or in custody. That leaves you two. We are investigating a number of known agents including Godfrey's pals Kim Philby and John Cairncross. We have some leads to some undersecretaries but we have no concrete evidence to back up our suspicions. That brings me to why I am here." Freddy was ahead of him in thinking that they were to be the carrots to be dangled as Sir George continued "We need your help to flush out whoever is the director. Our two main suspects are two undersecretaries and I am sending some selective information to them. One will be given correct information and one will receive a distraction. With your agreement I am going to tell them both that you have some Russian papers not yet disclosed to us, some that you collected from the Cuban flight.  It may of course be a little dangerous so I am asking you before I set things in motion and give out the information. Their agents have been very quiet since Bellinger died but we have news of some great event being planned by them and it is imminent. We have to take action very quickly." Freddy gave his reassurance "You can rely on me Sir." "Good man, get a good night's sleep and I will see you at my office in the morning at nine-o-clock." Freddy arrived in good time at the ministry office and was shown straight in. "Good morning Huntley do come in. Let me introduce you to Sir James Robert undersecretary from the ministry." Freddy shook hands. "I have been discussing with Sir James about these papers of yours. Do tell how you came to have these papers with information on Russian agents in the U.K." Sir George was relying on Freddy's ingenuity and discretion to play the charade with Sir James. Freddy duly went through the story of their escape from the Cuban air flight and how they found a lot of papers all in Russian. He failed to give the actual details of their method of escape and he wasn't sure why he kept that information from him. He told Sir James that he still had some of the papers that contained names and information that he had not yet handed over to Sir

George as they were still being translated. Freddy finished by saying "If you want I can get them to you sometime tomorrow Sir George." "That would be fine Huntley," agreed Sir George "how do intend to get them to me?" "I can bring them to your office in the morning." Sir George turned to Sir James "That seems to be a good idea. Well let's go to your club Sir James for an early brunch. That will be all Huntley, until tomorrow." He was leading Freddy by the arm to the office door and once out of earshot of Sir James he said "Well done Freddy I'll be in touch later today at your apartment if that is ok?" "I'll look forward to it Sir." Freddy left the ministry and set off back to the Italian restaurant below his apartment for a welcome cup of Italian coffee. Mario was one of the younger boys at the restaurant and his duties were to invite and greet people outside. Mario saw Freddy returning and greeted him warmly, showing him to a table in the window. Freddy sat with his coffee overlooking the Thames and watching the boats on the river and the people pass by. He thought about the challenges ahead and hoped that Sir George had reliable security people capable of keeping him safe. Sir George had been true to his word and set up a Huntley Haverstock bank account, credit cards and ministry top priority passes. On checking his new account it contained more money than he had ever dreamed of. He and Pinky had lunch in the downstairs restaurant and Pinky set off for the city. Freddy went up to his apartment and saw ahead of him Sir George making his way up the stairs. They went into the apartment together. "Well done this morning you handled it very well. If Sir James is our man then I don't think that he suspected a thing and swallowed your story hook, line and sinker. You are now in great danger if that is the case and Sir James contacts his Russian agents. You need to be armed and we will protect you as well as we can. You have had weapons training I asume during your training so a hand gun will not be new to you. I am taking you to the boffins to familiarise you with some gadgets and a new bullet proof car. You'll like this sporty new model, let's go." Sir George's car was outside waiting and they set off for the Boffin's secret building near Whitehall. They turned into a private garage entry that opened up  to reveal a covered interior quadrangle packed with cars and other vehicles. They went upstairs to an office and Freddy was introduced to Rupert who was in charge of field weapons development. Rupert was a dour character who was fully absorbed in his work which left a lot to be desired on the subject of people skills. On  introduction Rupert walked to the office door without acknowledging Freddy in any way. Rupert led them both to a very large upstairs workshop and spent most of the afternoon explaining in detail a variety of gadgets and the special features of his new bullet proof sports car. When Freddy drove up to the Italian restaurant following the ordeal that had been time with Rupert there was a parked car outside waiting for his return. The waiting car driver got out of his car and came over to Freddy "Huntley Haverstock?" Freddy nodded. "We are to take you to see the Home Secretary. Here is my I.D. You can follow us in your car if you wish." "I'll do that." Freddy replied. He was conscious that they may not be what they claimed to be. The cars were parked and he was actually taken to see the Home Secretary. "Huntley Haverstock?" the Home Secretary enquired. "Yes Sir." "I understand that you have now joined the service from the R.A.F. and you have already been on mission to Berlin?" "Yes sir." Freddy agreed. "What was all that about lad?" Freddy thought that that was a strange question to come from a Home Secretary. He also did not like the way that he was being questioned. Something was not as it should be here. Freddy answered "We were following a Russian double agent Godfrey Bellinger." "Are yes and he escaped into East Berlin no doubt?" He looked as if he did not know about the outcome in Berlin. "No sir he was shot and killed by a German security officer in a shootout." The Home Secretary was visibly shocked and then very angry. "Welcome to the service. That will be all." He turned and left the office leaving Freddy to find his own way out. Freddy got back to his car and drove the few blocks along Whitehall to Sir George's ministry office. Freddy explained to him the events of the visit to the Home Secretary but he didn't say anything about his personal impressions. "I do believe that the Home Secretary knew nothing about what happened in Berlin." Freddy said. "No I told no one hoping that someone would let us know that they knew. However the Russian agents being held in Berlin have been in custody longer than we expected and so the other side will not have been told. "Thank you for letting me in on this I'm sure that the Home Secretary will be on my back complaining about not being told. I'll tell him that the memo sent from Berlin at the time must have gone astray, mislaid or misdirected or something such. I'll be in touch with you in the morning." Freddy and Pinky spent the evening in town and Pinky told Freddy about the arrangements that had been made for him to retire back in his home town.

Pinky would be leaving early in the morning and so they had a farewell drink together tonight. Freddy was sorry that Pinky did not want to stay in London but he did have family back home and as far as he knew they must think that he was dead. It wasn't fair to let them continue with that thought. They spent  their final evening together discussing events and reminiscing about their R.A.F. lives together. They did not stay out too late and they had a final meal  together  in  the  Italian  restaurant.  The restaurant owners were also sorry to hear that Pinky was leaving.  The following morning before going to see Sir George they said their goodbyes and Pinky headed for his home town. Freddy went to deliver the nonexistent papers to Sir George and the whole thing went off without incident. "Well that clears those two chaps. Nothing happened with either of the set ups. If the opposition knew what had been discussed they would have moved heaven and earth to stop you passing such delicate information to me. We are back to square one Huntley." "Maybe not sir." said Freddy  and he related his feelings and impressions with regard to the meeting of the Home Secretary. "You cannot be serious. We can't start an investigation into the affairs of the Home Secretary, the press would be on it like a rocket and it would be public knowledge within hours. It would cause such serious repercussions that we could not risk it even if you are right." Sir George exclaimed. "We could set the same trap for him that we set for the other two. News of that will not be general knowledge. We could send him a memo telling him that I will be delivering the papers to you in a couple of hour's time. We have nothing to lose and it would at the least satisfy my suspicions." "I don't know if we could get away with it but as you say at this stage what have we to lose. Too much is at stake and time is short. Thinking about it, he is informed of all operations, well nearly all of them. He does have the knowledge and the opportunity to disclose information. Very well I'll send it right away by hand with time set at mid day." Freddy left the office and spent the next hour and a half considering what could and might happen. He hoped that Sir George had sufficient resources to deal with any trouble that could occur. As the appointed time approached he went to his car and set off to meet Sir George. He noticed a car set off behind him driving in the same direction. He turned past the Houses of Parliament and into Whitehall. The car followed and as he prepared to turn into the security building car park a car intercepted him and stopped directly in front of him. The following car stopped behind him blocking any attempt to escape in his car. The front car's doors were flung open and four men aimed their firearms directly at Freddy. Freddy froze as he sat trapped in his car. Suddenly, as if from nowhere, armed men surrounded the three cars and their occupants. Warning shots were fired and the raiders dropped their weapons and were taken into custody. People passing by thought that it must be a film set and applauded as the men were taken into custody and looked around wondering if they were themselves on camera. Freddy got out of his car and Sir George walked towards him. "You okay?" he asked and Freddy nodded "It looks as if you were right after all. The only thing now to do is to confront the Home Secretary but it is a delicate situation. We could have a national crisis on our hands." Freddy replied "We have no choice sir, he is a liability and still dangerous and as soon as he finds out what happened here you could be next on his hit list." "We will go alone you and I, that way we will not attract any unwanted attention." Sir George concluded. They walked together along Whitehall and straight up to the Home Secretary's office. As they went they brushes aside all challenges and walked unannounced into the Home Secretary's room. "What is the meaning of this Curswell?" The two men  in his office were told by Sir George to wait outside. The Home Secretary who had put all attention onto Sir George suddenly realised that Freddy was behind him and the shock registered on his face. "Yes sir it is Huntley Haverstock and he is alive and well. No doubt you did not expect to ever see him again. "Er, yes I met him here this morning to welcome him to the service." Sir George interrupted him "Yes and then you ordered him to be taken by your friends. They are now in custody and singing like song birds." "What nonsense is this?" he blustered but it showed on his face that he wasn't so confident. Sir George continued "You know full well what this is about. You have led a group of Russian agents who have been infiltrated into the senior positions in many of Her Majesties administrative services. Many of these infiltrators have been identified and dealt with, some severely. You will announce that you are taking a short break and come with us." Sir George picked up the phone and ordered a car. "You have no proof and you can't get away with this." The Home Secretary objected but not very convincingly. "You will find that we can do and have done. We do have proof and we will collect further proof very soon. You are under arrest and you will be taken into custody. Special service agents had been called and they led him from his office and the two men found in his office were also taken for questioning. The Prime Minister was informed of events and he gave instructions on the best way to deal with a very delicate situation. The media must not be allowed to get hold of any knowledge of it. All must be hush-hush, he told Sir George. The offices and London home of the Home Secretary were searched for evidence but it was only when his country residence was searched did they find complete listings, locations and functions of all of the Russian infiltrators. It was all the evidence that they needed. Operation 'Clean Sweep' was quickly put into action and within hours nearly all those on the lists were in custody. The number of senior posts that were held by infiltrators was more than anyone had expected. After a massive enquiry and much vetting completed, Sir George sat in his office satisfied that everything in the corridors of power was now under control. A modicum of trust could return to the ministry but they must be alert to the possibility that a future attempt to replace the lost agents might occur.

After his short break from his office the Home Secretary announced that he was stepping down because of a medical condition. The Prime Minister accepted his resignation and the media had a field day on speculation about his replacement. Sometime later the Home Secretary disappeared and was believed to have been seen in the company of the K.G.B.

Many agents were exchanged at the bridge at Friedrich Strasse, Check Point Charlie, including the defection to the West of Werner Stiller. He had continued to help to identify others following the help given to find Bellinger. In Sir George's office he spoke to Freddy "Well done Freddy or should I now say Huntley. You opened Pandora's Box with your German antics and whoever would have thought that it would lead to what it did. There will be a 'Gong' in this coup for me in the near future and I am certain that you Huntley will be highly decorated for your outstanding contribution to national security. I would be very disappointed if you chose to leave us now. You have every right to if you choose but I do hope that you remain with us." "Thank you sir, I can't see myself doing anything else now. I would be delighted to remain in the service." Freddy accepted. I am very pleased and I can now tell you that you are to be promoted to the rank of Commander and you will be sent for full training to fit you for your appointment. You will be away for some time but I look forward to your return." They shook hands in true respect and friendship. Freddy was soon sent to special traing and spent a lot of time in different countries familiarising himself with traditions and various activities associated with them. After many months of training he returned to London to take up active service but first he was due a lot of leave and he decided to take a sabbatical in his home town. He felt that after loosing his identity he needed to try to pick up the threads of his life again.

And so ends the story of Freddy Goodchild for now but the story of Huntley G. Haverstock now begins.

## Author's Note:

All events and stories in this book are pure fiction and no event or action can be attributed to any person living or dead.

## Note:

The position of Home Secretary did not exist in 1962 hence the story bears no reference to any person living or dead.

## <u>Huntley Haverstock Returns</u>

Following the sixties spy scandal and the Cuba crisis, Huntley Haverstock returned to his former life as Freddy Goodchild. During his involvement in the 'D' notice affair with Cuba and the foreign spies, all records of Freddy's existence had been destroyed by the foreign agents. The British Secret Services had restored his records following extensive investigations.

Freddy and his friend Master pilot Pinky James had given the secret services tremendous help in exposing infiltrators who had managed to establish themselves in many British Government departments. Only the government offices had any record of the help that they had given, it could never be in the public domain. Freddy did however hold an M.B.E. for outstanding courage and contribution to Her Majesties government. Many infiltrators in the Government services had been identified and arrested around the time of the Cuban crisis and many new security measures had been introduced. It was hoped that the new measures would prevent any such infiltration in the future. Freddy's help at that time had been invaluable and was the main reason for his recognition. He had remained with the secret services for some time following that affair and had been trained and promoted in the service. He had been involved in a number of investigations but none as serious as his first. It seemed a long time after his joining the service and he was due leave. He was subject to recall as Huntley Haverstock when the service required him. It was a long time since he had seen his family who had believed him dead but unbeknown to Freddy his family had died in that time. The family were led to believe that Freddy had died because when they enquired about him they were told that was no record of anyone of that name. He was now taking his leave and travelling home to Middlesbrough wondering what lay ahead on taking up his earlier life. As he left London on his way to Middlesbrough he reflected that his circumstances were now totally different as he was now very wealthy and had the means to do what might have been unthinkable before. He travelled up the A1 in his Aston Martin DB4GT 'jet coupe' enjoying his 0-60miles per hour acceleration in 6.4 seconds. It was very gratifying to think that his wealth had mainly come from the people who had tried to kill him. He hadn't heard from family or friends but had had contact with his former R.A.F. associates. As he drove through the driving rain he realised that he was quite nervous and apprehensive as he approached his home town.

Middlesbrough was an "Iron" town, built on the local requirements of the Dorman and Long steel works. Previous to the steel works the town was a half way stage between Whitby Abbey and Durham Cathedral. Monks would rest there on there journeys between the Priories and access the ferry across the Tees river. "Would his house still be there or had it been sold off by the family?" "What would the family think when he walked in on them?" these were just a few of the things that haunted him as he pulled up outside of his house in Linthorpe. The rain had eased to a fine drizzle as he walked up the path and stopped outside of his front door. For the first time he had a look at the frontage, the windows were covered by metal sheets and the door was sealed up by boards screwed into the door frame. A sign read,

## 'DANGER DO NOT ENTER'.

Freddy was not going to be told that he could not enter his own house, no matter who had put up the sign. Freddy was in shock as he slowly went back to his car to get a tyre lever and as he approached the front door he wondered if his keys would still fit or had the locks been changed as well. He prised the board off across the lock and tried his key, it turned and he pushed the door open.

The door resisted from lack of use but as it opened the smell from inside stung his nostrils and sent him reeling backwards. He covered his face with a handkerchief as he levered off the remaining boards from the door frame and he entered the house. Not one bit of furniture was left in the house, everything had been removed and the house was littered with smashed pots, flower jars, ornaments and paperwork. The house had been totally emptied of furniture and carpets. It looked as if looters had cleared the place of everything of use. What was that smell? The downstairs rooms had the appearance of desolation with dirt and mess spread all over the floors. What had happened here? After searching upstairs as well as down he eventually looked in the cupboard under the stairs and his gaze was met by a hollow eyed corpse in an advanced state of decomposition. He was shocked but there seemed to be something familiar about it, the stained clothing indicated that whoever this was had been shot or stabbed in the stomach and left to die a slow death trapped under the stairs. Freddy checked the clothing for any identification but there was nothing.